LIASION

Part 3
Affairs of the Heart ~ Hollywood

KEW TOWNSEND

Tremmelle Publishing

HOLLYWOOD, CALIFORNIA

Affairs of the Heart
Hollywood Series

BLOOD (Part 1)
SURRENDER (Part 2)
DECEPTION (Part 4)

Affairs of the Heart
London Series

HEART (Part 1)
TEMPTATION (Part 2)
PROMISES (Part 3)
DEVOTED (Part 4)
BETRAYAL (Part 5)

Sign up for NEWSLETTER
kewtownsend.com

CONTENTS

Chapter One

NOWHERE TO RUN

1989
Six days — Kaine

Christmas Day
Holly Hill's Home
West Hollywood, California

Words blew over Holly Hill's face.

"Then marry me," Luka Hunter challenged.

Holly collapsed back onto the bed after the powerful lovemaking. Every muscle in her body was blown to the other side of Oblivion, a place she visited often. The dream words echoed in her mind.

— *Then marry me.*

When she regained her strength, she looked at Luka.

He repeated the words, "Will you, Babe? Marry me?"

"Isn't this a bit premature? There is one problem." She warned barely able to speak not because the words came from out of the blue.

"What? I will move mountains if you say yes."

"Well, in this case, the mountain is Mount Tessa. You're already married!"

"Not for long. As soon as I'm free, will you marry me straightaway?"

Holly wanted to say yes after their explosive night. There would no longer be a future with Kaine Walker, her beautiful and romantic time traveler and frontman for the super band *Hurrikaine*. Kaine once thought she'd slept with Luka Hunter and called her 'Luka's whore.' Well, she was now. Though to be accurate, the term should be mistress. *Luka's mistress* and the words rattled in her head. Not a description she would ever think to define herself.

"I ... I'm ... not positive... if ... I ... can ..." she said not knowing how to stop him.

Luka's usual sunny smile cooled as she lay in his arms.

"You can, and you will."

She started to explain that she couldn't marry him for many reasons. But mostly because she carried Kaine's child, and that the love she'd screamed in passion didn't reflect her heart.

But Luka Hunter refused to listen. He'd continued before she spoke.

"What you don't understand is — you're mine. And when I say that, I don't mean in the possessive sense. I mean that contractually, I manage you, and I'm involved in every facet of your professional career. I'm also *The Heart of Hollywood's* producer, your show, for which I have you under contract.

"I also have the final say about what reaches airtime. Personally, we've been romantically linked to the bloody awful Malibu photos as lovers due to the tabloids cover our every move together.

"To marry me solves the rest of the problems. Your child will be considered mine, no bloody problem there. Given our history, I 'expect' you to accept my marriage proposal straightaway ... the next time I bloody well ask you."

"And if I say ... no...?"

"But you won't, will you?"

A single eyebrow rose, and the sparkle in his eyes vanished, replaced with a new message that said 'don't ever cross me.' And, he'd made it clear what her future held for her. She'd become the pawn for him to move about, as he wanted. And yes, Kaine's words stated the same thing about Luka.

I'm just the king pawn for him to move about.

One man, held the controlling stock in Cable Music Television, (CMT), at fifty-one percent, Luka Hunter, the most powerful man on cable television in the music world with no one powerful enough to stop him.

"Let's bloody well stop all this negative chatting. It's Christmas my beauty."

Later, Holly lay in a twilight sleep with Luka's arms wrapped around her. His hands cupped her breasts. She'd had a restless sleep. Kaine arrived to taunt her in her dreams and his face filled with disappointment and accusations. But Luka's steady breathing forced the dream lover to show respect for her. The flesh and blood of Luka moved up her back growing like a snake. When fully alive he wanted her, and Kaine's shadow slithered into the dark fog of her dreams, waiting for her to return to sleep to torment her.

By mid-morning, Christmas day, Luka had other plans. She'd learned quickly to enjoy his incredibly sensual and insatiable moods. In fact, Luka unrestrained turned out to be something to reckon with and needed to pace herself. His talent and fortitude challenged her to keep up with him. Her pride would never let allow him the satisfaction that she barely hung on for dear life. She predicted Luka to be wonderful first thing in the morning, especially Christmas morning. He should be a wonderful present.

But wasn't.

His cool fingers held her breasts, pulling her close to him, oh so close. He lay lazily rocking inside her. It should be a perfect way to awaken Christmas morning. He should be the perfect gift, especially since he never finished, only when he'd said.

But he wasn't.

She drifted back into a light sleep and ran headlong into Kaine waiting for her. His stern expression told her to stop this ridiculous affair right now! He'd planned to take her away in a few days. His words clear — end the affair.

The father of your child is coming for you!

Holly awoke startled, in a sweat, waking Luka. He took it as a sign to start again. She relaxed. Kaine vanished not wishing to be a third party to her lovemaking.

Holly had no place to be on Christmas day. She should be satisfied this would be the pattern of her day. That she would lay with Luka, quenching his never ceasing appetite, a willing captive hungry for him.

But she wasn't.

She wasn't willing — only obedient.

He finally lay quiet.

She looked at his full succulent lips red from kissing and sucking every part of her body. His lips were partly open as if he invited her tongue to search the familiar depth of his mouth. His powerful hands held her tight. Oh, those magical fingers that caressed and massaged, slipping in and out and all around her body each time as if he'd never been there before bringing her new delight and pleasure. And when she thought his passion too much, he showed her a new position and new way to experience his deep penetration, as if in his mind, he flipped through the Kama Sutra page-by-page.

Luka attempted to exhaust his tricks in his bag of magic to make her body beg for more. She listened to Luka say he loved her thousands of different ways and the places he wanted to take her. The dreams he shared with her even brought her to tears a few times. But he hadn't said he loved her.

But she needed to convince him — she did.

Especially since the ghost of Kaine, not dead, as she expected, but exiled to the other side of the ocean, visited her while she slept every chance he got. It would stay her secret, her love for him in her heart, his ghost vibrant and alive. Incredibly real moments, as if Kaine sat watching them, watching her, become Luka's whore. He stole all the joy and pleasure Luka openly lavished on her.

Hell was still living between these two men.

Why did Kaine coming to her, bringing his love so strong it almost materialized in her small cottage? She couldn't run — she couldn't hide.

Luka must have sensed her dilemma because he hugged her to put her at ease.

"It is okay Babe. You're not alone anymore. I'm real and much stronger than ghosts."

She smiled. Yes, but where was the relief because he'd read her mind perfectly? Did Luka sneak into her dreams to watch Kaine as well? They belonged together her and Luka. Supposed to be their future. Luka left her no other choice. She should be happy with Luka, overjoyed by his devotion and extraordinary love for her.

But she wasn't.

Holly was cautious and wary. His demand that she says yes to his proposal the next time he'd asked had sounded too much like a threat. A threat that might cause harm to her and the child she carried if she denied him.

She decided to move slowly with Luka. Her legal training encouraged her to as she worked on a plan, thinking of loopholes to break her binding contracts with him. And then how she would put distance between her and the always magnetic Mr. Hunter.

Out of nowhere, Luka shook her from her mysterious thoughts.

"Babe! Wake up! I'm due at Michael's in an hour. I bloody forgot he's having a Christmas brunch, and I need to be there. Come on, I want you with me," he encouraged. His facial expression happy, his eyes glowing — all of him glowed. Could she call it love? Yes, Luka Hunter was lost in the throes of love but afraid to say the words. He'd asked her to marry him, but it didn't make up for not saying the all-important phrase. He reached over and slapped her bare derrière.

"What about opening presents?"

"Would you be too disappointed if we did that when we come back home?" He quickly added.

Home. She heard the word.

Luka gave her what she needed that he would come back 'home' with her. She wouldn't be free of him or his sexual curiosity today. With the glorious Dream compound Luka lived in, he seemed to prefer her tiny nest to hang his hat.

She jumped at the urgent sting of his insistence again on her bottom.

"Come on, I want my Christmas angel with me." Luka leaned over near her face, his breath freshly scented with peppermint, and as he kissed her, he popped a mint into her mouth, and they passed it back and forth.

Moments later when she stared into his sparkling blue eyes, he confessed.

"Who would bloody well expected you and me this happy?"

She cuddled real close, Luka's Mistress used her words.

"Speaking of which, how am I supposed to keep myself at a professional distance? How am I supposed to hide my insatiable desire you've awakened in me? I'm positive it's blazing in my eyes. Everyone will notice, and I'll be embarrassed."

He cheerfully scooped her up in his arms and hugged her tightly. The tall length of his body filled her curves. She marveled at Luka standing naked.

His chest expanded and then he exhaled with a tiny chuckle.

"That's one of the reasons I love you, Babe. Women

always liked to display me as a trophy or expensive ornament.

"But not you.

"You're embarrassed you have feelings for me, powerful feelings of a woman in love. A woman deeply in love, and you can't hide it, judging by the last few hours."

He kissed her neck and then pushed her hair from her eyes.

Yes, she caught the words *I love you.* Easily slipped into the reasons he loved her. How long would she wait for those words to stand-alone?

She hoped she'd be long gone.

Luka continued to look straight into her eyes. "It's okay Babe, to be in love with me. Fuck!" he exclaimed slapping himself on the forehead. "I got to give you permission to bloody love me? It's okay. Love me. Show it. I won't ever refuse you. I'm not Kaine. I promise I won't hurt you, ever."

He'd said the word.

Kaine.

That upset her but was relieved he'd said he would never hurt her. Perhaps she'd overreacted to his passionate confession about his expectations for their relationship. He must have sensed the dip in her spirit because he paused and took a step closer.

"I'm here. You can come to me. Touch me, kiss me, I'm real. I will always want to sleep with you and wake up to you. Can't you tell?"

He took her hand and pressed it against his stiff love.

"And if we can't take being apart, we'll leave early, come back here and I'll show you more tricks until we can't move."

She laughed. "I can't see you ever *that* satisfied."

"I'm willing to see what it takes?" He admitted and smiled his sexy Luka smile.

How simple he made it sound. It should have been no more games.

No pretending.

No Kaine!

It should have been that they adored and cherished each other and let it show.

But it wasn't.

Holly wondered how much emotion should show to keep her and the baby safe, but she would learn. For the time being, she needed to follow her plan to convince Luka that she cared as much for him as he seemingly did for her.

Luka pulled on her hand, dragging her from her thoughts and led her to the shower. The water flowed warm and refreshing.

He leaned her up against the shower wall, and he dropped to his knees and placed his hot lips on her, pulled her swollen lips apart and quickly took charge. He placed one leg on his shoulder moving in even closer and gave her all the expertise of his travels until she could take no more of the exquisite pleasure and blurted.

"You're wonderful," while her body released.

Luka stood and whispered, "You taste good," then kissed her over the peaking pleasure. His fingers entered and pumped her to the signpost ahead — Oblivion.

Chapter Two

SECRET LOVERS

Holly lay limp in his arms.

Luka seized a condom from the edge of the sink determined to bring her back for more, showing her the fun showering with him. There seemed to be no end to his imagination. And when he'd finished, she tingled.

Luka washed her hair and then while he rinsing instructed.

"The next time you're keen to do something like, say, cut your hair. Please check and ask me first."

"You? Why would I check with you?"

"Because everything you do affects your image. In this case, your hair looks beautiful and compliments your face. But on any other decisions, please consult with me first."

Holly couldn't let him see her surprise or the indignity from his intrusion into her personal care.

"Of course, how thoughtless of me that I didn't think about how it would affect my image."

"Well, luckily, the camera loves your face and your hair won't change that."

Holly remained dumbfounded but delivered enough strength to return the pampering by lathering his hair and then rinsed. Afterward, as if a reward, he kissed her long she thought she would be permanently sealed to him. She broke the kiss.

He grabbed the last condom.

"Again, Luka?" Hoping he'd back away.

"Michael can wait." Luka took over pressing her against the wall. He wrapped her legs up around his waist as she held onto his neck.

"I like fucking ... ah, making love to you Babe. You fit perfectly."

Use your words. "I like fucking you too Luka."

"Babe? You're using profanity." He chuckled as he moved in deeper, strong, physical, and powerful.

Holly smiled at him while dressing after the hot, steamy shower picturing his astonishing love tactics. Perhaps she should relax and make the best of this situation. He did love her and would take good care of her.

Holly decided to say. "Luka I'm not convinced I can go to Michael's. To be separated from you may prove to be hard to do."

"Hard? Babe, it's impossible for me to be away from you. To look at you makes me remember how hot, wet, and tight you are. That makes me hard, and I want to be inside you this instant."

She smiled appreciating his directness. He continued to teach her to use her words of seduction outside of the bed. How equally powerful they worked.

"To look at you makes me wet too," she confirmed using her words. She recognized her effectiveness with instant rewards from him.

He warned quickly. "Don't Babe, or we'll never get out of here."

He did make her wet since the first moment she'd seen him at the airport in London. And thinking of all the tricks he shared with her, she sighed. It would be at least two long hours at Michael Richmond's, CEO of Cable Music Television, and her boss. Well, that might be a stretch, as Luka was the silent boss in charge of everything, owning most of CMT.

The drive both ways from her cozy cottage in the canyon, above the Sunset Strip, to Bel-Air, would kill her sensual mood. She calculated time spent with the obligatory visit to the Richmond home, added it up, and determined she could avoid his touch for at least three or four hours.

"What?" he said, throwing her a smile as he pulled his shirt out to cover the bulge in his pants?

"I want you constantly," she admitted.

Luka laughed then gave her a sweet smile.

"Those are words I've waited to hear from you for such a long time. But we have a small situation. I have to go straightaway for a little while."

She almost asked why. Luka didn't owe anything to Michael. Michael worked for Luka as they all did! She sighed. Luka would tell her when ready that he held the controlling interest in CMT.

They moved fast. They were late. The inventive love making in the shower took too long. Luka didn't have a clue to the meaning of the word *quickie*. After a hasty stop at the Dream compound to change clothes, he maniacally drove through the streets of West Hollywood heading for Michael's mansion in the star-studded Bel-Aire.

Holly wore beige, double-breasted Asset suit with a short mini skirt, Tessa insisted she buy because it would hide her paunch for a few months until she could diet it away. It would take more than a few meals of lettuce to whittle down this paunch. She'd spent the Thanksgiving holiday with this warm and inviting family, therefore, she no longer reacted as a stranger, and Holly easily fit in with the elegantly dressed Catherine. Michael looked every inch a CEO. Even Keith and Crissy, their teenagers, dressed for the occasion given up their casual look they'd sported in Wyoming. A few guests mingled around a large crystal bowl of spiked eggnog.

When Holly entered on Luka's fashionable arm, everyone turned to look. Were they impressed? He wore a light blue Asset suit with a crisp white, button down, banded-collared shirt. His blonde, shiny hair brushed back and secured at the nape of his neck. Or, admiring the next GQ cover model, her sophisticated and handsome lover? She might be seeing more than what everyone else did, but he seemed to glow.

Catherine greeted Holly and Luka with a warm hostess smile. But it seemed laced with an inquiring tone. "What a handsome couple you make. You're positively glowing ... any announcements yet?"

Holly's face flushed a bright rose in her cheeks.

Luka answered as he squeezed Holly's hand meaningfully.

"You'll be the first we'll tell," he promised, passing a knowing wink to Catherine. Then he asked, "Catherine, please entertain Holly? I believe Michael's waiting for me?"

Luka gave Holly another squeeze of her hand.

"I won't be gone for long. Can you hold out?" He teased as he whispered the last words into her hair and kissed her ear.

"Maybe, maybe not," she replied, smiling and raising her eyebrows, hoping he thought she might not.

Catherine escorted Holly into the massive living room and introduced her to a few movie types and generic music industry guest. But Catherine wanted to chat.

Holly looked over at her and inquired. "Do I still have that starved cat look?"

"No, I'd say you're hungry, but not starved. Anything you want to tell me?"

Catherine motioned to follow her out to their well-manicured garden, the kind Holly came to expect in luxurious Bel-Aire. Catherine motioned for Holly to sit next to her on a rattan settee and anxiously asked. "Are you going to tell me what's going on with you?"

"There's not much to tell. Luka wants to marry me. How? He's married to Tessa! I'd say it's a pretty confusing and complicated situation."

And what she didn't say, she hadn't accepted his proposal and quietly waited for the baby's real father due in a few days and expected to reconcile with her.

But Catherine's instincts ran high. "Are you all right with this setup?"

"For a while," Holly sighed. "There's not too much that can be changed. For the time being, yes, things are fine."

"Are you aware that when you look at Luka, you glow? You have since I first met you."

Taken aback, Holly tried to hold back a big smile.

"I have? I never realized."

She was going to say she hadn't comprehended that she'd always been in way over her head with him.

What she did say, "As transparent as that?"

Who else was a witness?

Everyone else saw her swallowed up by her intense attraction for Luka. Kaine hadn't missed it that was for sure! Again, the instant pain from the pinch of guilt, followed by hot embarrassment and next ... betrayal.

"I didn't think you understood how far in you are. I've seen it many times with young people. And you, in love with him at Thanksgiving in Sheridan with all the signs there. I hoped the rocky road wouldn't stop you from staying together."

"What do you mean?"

"I mean Kaine."

Holly flashed her classic look of, 'you knew?'

"Of course. The world waits to see what will happen with the *Heart of the Hurrikaine*, except I have a secret, she loves Luka."

But she didn't and what she said, "Well, I'm at liberty to say it's official. Luka told me I'm allowed to love him."

Catherine laughed. "That's our Luka. If you need anything, a friend to talk to, I'd like it if you considered me that friend and confidant. Michael and I are fond of you and Luka, and we wish you both every happiness."

Then Catherine smiled and leaned in to hug her and returned to the other guests.

A loud commotion came from the living room. To Holly's surprise, Santa delivered a hearty, "Ho, Ho, Ho," and then appeared.

Santa pushed through the front door and sat down next to the ceiling-high Christmas tree. All the guest's children flocked around Santa that started to hand out presents to their squeals of delight. It seemed odd that Santa should speak with a decidedly crisp British accent. Where there no end to Luka's surprises? She watched him playing with the kids, sensitive and genteel. However, would he make the best father for Kaine's son?

When Santa passed, he whispered to her.

"Little girl, will you come and sit on Santa's lap and tell him who you want for Christmas?"

She laughed heartily, obligingly followed. "I've already been given the greatest present I would want."

"Well, maybe if you ask Santa real nice, he'll give it to you again." And he winked at her.

"Right behind you Santa," as she trailed him to the back of the mansion to the pool house. There, Michael had kept the fur-trimmed red suit safely out-of-sight from the children. Santa pulled his beard from his face securing it below his chin. He embraced Holly and kissed her as if she was a dying man's last wish. He was starved for her. And it looked like Santa was going to make his wish come true.

How much time passed made it difficult to gauge, but clearly, Luka would not make love here. She kissed him until the urgency passed. He pulled away. His eyes hung hooded and glazed but mostly glassy from lust. Santa Luka, such a visual turn-on. She hung on to her last breath and conceded.

"They will see how bewitched I'm about you when I walk in, this time, Santa. How I can't keep my hands off you."

He laughed. "It is okay Babe, smashing. Let them all fucking see. Let them see I can make you happy." He slipped out of the Santa suit.

The sight of him naked proved to be more than she could bear. She playfully lunged toward him. As she reached out for him, he lightly slapped her teasing hand a few times. His body responded, fully aroused, and would need immediate attention if she pursued her task.

Luka knew it. It was then his heart-breaking words slipped out.

"I see why Kaine is besotted with you."

The words, not meant to be cruel on the surface, stabbed at her guilty heart. He'd cut too deep. Why did he speak that name?

Her heart bled, and she sank into the chair. Her mind reeled reeling with thoughts, jumping to conclusions. The rage and anger soon proved to be stronger than her rational mind, and she rose with the speed of a rocket, lambasting Luka with a string of words even she couldn't understand.

In the end, she screamed at him.

"You do? You've been with me all this time, trying to figure out what the hell Kaine saw in me?"

Her outrage poured out strong and couldn't control herself. All the months of torment and his recent demand that she accept his marriage proposal the next time he asked, obviously piled up, became too much, and she exploded, yelling at him.

"You set me up, you bastard. Have I passed your tests? Has it all been a cruel, disgusting game for you to punish Kaine? Is it ... you bastard?"

Holly lunged screaming at him. When he didn't answer, she shouted.

"You bastard, how could you?"

At the same time, her hand connected with his smooth,

freshly shaven cheek. The force of the blow stung her hand as his hair secured in a tail, broke free, and swung

Chapter Three

IF I WERE A CARPENTER AND (YOU WERE A LADY)

Holly's hand burned as if she'd held it over a blazing fire. And her heart bled from his lacerating words. She automatically raised her hand to swing a second time. His hand caught her arm mid-air, blocking her sharp rebuttal.

"Babe, please. What a thoughtless thing for me to say. Please? Give me a bloody second to explain, please."

Her hot, stinging tears spilled down over her cheeks. The pain in Luka's eyes surprised her.

With no thought to the red swelling forming on his face, he took his fingertips and wiped away her falling tears.

"Those are the last tears I'll ever cause you."

Luka took her in his arms hugging her fiercely, rocking her, comforting her, cradling her head as he quickly explained in her ear.

"What I meant to say. Can you hear me?"

She sighed and let him hold her, doing everything she could to keep her anger in check.

"Yes, I'm listening."

"Good, keep listening to every word. Please?"

She nodded her head, the anger melting as his arms swaddled her.

"What I meant, and should have said. Remember what I told you in London about Kaine, women, and I. Kaine can have any socialite, whore, groupie, any woman he wants. Yet he wanted you, why? That's a perfectly reasonable question.

"The facts are women want men like Kaine and me. We're high profile, successful and wealthy beyond reason. They think one way to us is through sex, but not you Babe. You're sincere that when you playfully came after me, I knew you were after *me*. Not keeping up a pretense to see what you can get. It wasn't 'Luka Hunter, and what he could give to you.' You treat me as if I could be in any line of work and you would love me. Kaine found this with you too.

"And Babe, it's the greatest compliment in the world. To be a man and loved and desired by his woman for himself. Especially, in this fucked up music business world, I come from, Babe.

"Do you understand?

"What I meant?

"Kaine's in my head too. He was closer to me than any brother could be. And we did what Caesar and Alexander dreamed of doing. We conquered the entire bloody world together. He's on my mind too."

Holly looked up into Luka's crisp blue eyes. Yes, she saw a tiny bit of weakness. She leaned in and apologetically kissed his cheek where the blood recently rushed. It puffed out his skin and left a large red welt exactly the size and shape of her hand.

"You also had a bloody hell right to react as you did," he acknowledged, smiling to bring a touch of levity to the dark moment rubbing his welt.

She stood quietly for a moment.

"Are you okay?" he asked softly.

Holly nodded, noting a mixture of remorse and foolish. She needed to get over these insecure feelings of being manipulated to make this complicated relationship with Luka work. She had to, for her health, and for the safety of her baby

Luka turned, dressed quickly and then reached for his jacket and slipped into it.

"Can you forgive me?" She asked to break the silence as they headed for the main house.

"I can forgive you anything." He pledged as a tiny smile curled about his lips.

She hoped he meant those words, unable to dismiss her anxious feelings, wondering what he'd do when Kaine came back and took her from him … again.

Would he forgive her, or would he kill her?

They stepped into the main room to a barrage of wisecracks.

"Santa got fresh with one of his elves and smacked him?" Michael teased.

She smiled sympathetically. It was the first time she'd seen Luka blush.

"What do we have?" Luka gruffly growled at Michael, changing the subject.

"Follow me to my study, I have it all ready."

"Babe, this includes you, come on," Luka instructed taking her arm at the elbow to follow Michael and entered his lavishly furnished study.

He headed for his mahogany desk where he picked up a fat eight-by-ten envelope.

"As you instructed, *Bon Jour's* playing Tucson, Arizona, tomorrow night. The CMT jet is ready to fly tonight at seven sharp. Here're the address and a map to the executive mansion.

"You have the drill down pat. Here's the company credit card and cash for expenses, etc. I'll have a video crew there tomorrow, early afternoon. Jaden's making himself available for interviews as a favor to you. Says you go way back. His people will contact with the time.

"You will be flying back to L.A., with the band on their plane. I think that covers it. Oh, Holly, I understand we have you to thank for this great idea. Keep them coming," Michael congratulated matter-of-factly as he sifted through another stack of papers and handed them to Luka.

Luka turned to Michael saying, "Brilliant, we're out of here. We have to pack for the desert."

As they headed down the long corridor, she turned to ask.

"What did he mean my idea? It was yours."

"I got the idea at your place because you played *Bon Jour*. You're my muse Babe, might as well get credit."

Holly shook her head as Luka pulled out his cellular phone, tucked down in his pocket, to answer for the first time since he'd arrived. His calls must have been forwarded again. Luka Hunter, an admittedly mysterious man, and one hell of an executive worked on Christmas day, putting another moneymaking promotion together. She decided she'd stop trying to figure him out and would kick back and let him do the driving. He would be anyway.

Holly ventured to wish Catherine a very Merry Christmas.

She found her instructing her maid on how to rearrange hors d'oeuvres on a platter in the kitchen. Catherine flashed a wide, friendly smile as Holly approached her.

"Holly, I wanted to mention that Luka's entirely different with you. I've never seen him so mellow and happy. I've also never seen him alive, whatever you're doing, don't stop."

The words came flowing back to haunt her. Words from before, in London, at Friar Manor, at the *Hurrikaine's* table when everyone commented on her fabulous effect on Kaine. She should bottle her strange and magical potion she'd used on these two powerful and lonely men. Something about her created a positive effect on them. She would have never anticipated judging by her simple life experiences with men before *Hurrikaine*. Perhaps they'd never met an unpretentious, down-to-earth lady.

Impossible.

But how healthy was this down-to-earth lady? After a few days with her, she watched Kaine have his heart broken and wounded him unimaginably, then ended up in drug rehabilitation at the castle. The long dark shadows of apprehension started their usual seepage into her thoughts.

What of her future with Luka?

Did she have one?

What would happen to Luka when Kaine came for her?

Who would be left standing?

Chapter Four

ISN'T IT A PITY

Holly and Luka had a few hours before the CMT jet left for Arizona. Luka drove Holly to the Dream compound first, and his houseman Pierce had packed up his desert clothes. Luka grabbed a warm coat, and he waited for her in his doorway.

Holly laid her hand on his chest dressed in a beige western shirt with covered snaps under her hand. She ran her fingertips up his black leather vest and hugged his beige Levi hips scraping her body on the jade belt buckle he wore.

Holly kissed him quickly.

Luka slipped on a tan Stetson cowboy hat shaking his long, angel hair to draped about his shoulders. He kissed her back while throwing his white, sheep-lined coat over his arm.

He took another step, and she noticed a turquoise bracelet and a thin turquoise necklace that hung next to the gold inscribed medallion, her Christmas gift to him. He looked ready to catch a plane for Nashville instead of Arizona.

Luka's kiss left the season's peppermint flavor on her

lips. She licked them and smiled at him.

"I wanted to tell you, Babe. This is the first time I've ever wanted to catch a flight. I have spent most of my life on airplanes and sitting in airports, surrounded by a bloody lot of rude, crude musicians and road crews. I'm bloody well sick of traveling with blokes. For the first time in my life, I'm genuinely happy to be back on the road. I've never traveled more than a few stops with groupies or female friends. It's great to be with you. I'm happy we are together. We're getting to be quite a jet-setting team, aren't we Babe? You can travel with me, make new dreams, and together, fulfill them. Do you trust me enough to tell me your dreams?"

"You're amazing Luka."

"You sound surprised? How could I accomplish anything without dreaming it up first?"

"You're amazing, my sweet angel eyes."

"I'm glad you've noticed." He sent her a wry smile.

It warmed her heart and encouraged her. Perhaps this trip would help Luka to open up and tell her about his dark, mysterious past and deadly secrets.

Luka leaned in and brushed her lips with his. He sent scorching heat to run through her as if a torch dropped in a barrel of gasoline and this wasn't the time to ravish him even though he'd intensely touched her heart with his sweet confession. She couldn't understand how his exciting life with the world's top rock acts could make him detest flying. How many adventures had he experienced these past ten years? How many ports of call did he remember? How many women had he bedded? She didn't want the answer to that question.

Presently, she held no book of details about him. The few news articles about business, always raving about his accomplishments, but nothing ever revealed his personal life, or even about his wife, Tessa. The nuggets of his past seemed far and few between in the media. She'd figure it out too late in the game what he'd wanted from her, and that started with trust.

Naturally, he wanted love, but it didn't top his list. No, the word trust sat in honor. Even after she'd betrayed him and left with Kaine for days in London, he'd forgiven her.

But did he trust her?

Perhaps?

Difficult to tell with his dancing blue eyes, if he trusted her, enough to tell her of the demons he must carry with him and let down the shield that covered his secrets.

Would he let her see the *real* Luka Hunter?

She sighed, looking at his perfect face and those luscious, succulent lips always begging to be kissed and promised herself soon.

Holly relaxed, ready to find out what life would be like on the road with Luka. And as cautious as she should be in these tenuous circumstances, she did trust Luka, reminding herself that he'd been there at every turn when trouble struck. And the new feelings she held for Luka simmered.

"I thought I'd spend Christmas night in your arms."

Luka released his Cheshire smile.

"I like when you tell me how you feel."

"It's impossible to hide."

His smile grew wide and generous, and when Luka smiled, the world lit up brightly.

"Like the first time we met," he admitted.

"I'm that transparent?"

"I looked down at you, helpless in my arms, your breath thick with English ale, your sexy body limp, and trusting. When you looked up at me, I fill with the greatest rush. You lit up, Babe. Those big brown eyes of yours devoured me as they are now. Your lips pursed as if waiting for me to kiss you forever, and truthfully, I would have fancied that. Don't you see? I'm a puppy in your hands."

"You have that effect on me too," she whispered.

"It will grow stronger," he promised as he threw her a generous smile.

"You've told me many times, but it's difficult to understand your attraction to me, I'm not different from other women."

"But you're refreshingly different — especially, last night. It's as I've explained to you. For the past fourteen years, I've never known what women wanted. It's never been for me! I can't complain women come with the job. And I promise I won't ever give you any reason to doubt my commitment to you. But after a few years, I gave up ever finding a woman who would love the real me."

"Does that include Carrin?" She might have well as slapped him again. She watched the shield close down over his face like the partition in a limo as he instantly locked away the pain behind his eyes.

Luka finished — through sharing. He kissed her quickly as if nothing happened, but it had. From Luka's point of view, Carrin held the honor to be the one woman to love him. Then fragmented pictures of her in Luka's arms flashed across her mind. How they had been together in England, Wyoming, California, and soon Arizona. How surprising, she thought the twists and turns in life.

Luka turned, picked up his suitcase, leaned in with his hands full, and kissed her deeply, and the leather from his vest smothered her in his masculinity. She wanted him. But they needed to get to her place.

Luka moved away, weaning her from his kiss with a quick succession of kisses and then advised.

"I think I have everything, I've got my passport, and you'll need to grab yours too. Always carry it with you from this point forward, Babe. You won't always have notice when we will need them to leave the country. Let's go, we haven't much time."

Luka drove like a race car driver to her place, taking the curves of Mulholland Drive a bit recklessly. While she held her breath, he filled her in about Jaden in *Bon Jour* and the shoot in Arizona.

Arriving at her door in one piece but frazzled, she discovered another guitar case. Holly ran her hand freely over the black hard shell. Luka followed her walking down the steps. She quickly brought in Kaine's latest message and stacked it in the closet with the others. She didn't dare take the time to read the card.

Luka followed after making room in his trunk for her already packed luggage she'd intended to take back east for the holiday to visit her parents, but the treacherous snowstorm grounded all planes on the East Coast. She stuffed the last guitar case in the full closet with the other guitar cases. He walked in as she shut the door.

"Well, Babe. It's Christmas, and I want you to open my presents."

Holly walked up to Luka, rested her hand on his chest,

and then moved up over his shoulder, up his warm neck to the nape of his hairline.

"I have presents enough when I look into your eyes and see how you want me."

Luka's eyes seem to brighten and then dimmed with a thin veil of red mist. Not a reaction she would have anticipated from him.

He pulled her into his arms and kissed her tenderly, telling her how much he loved her.

Lost in Luka's gentle kiss, her body responded to him, and her hand roamed his body.

Luka broke the kiss, pulling her down to the carpet by her hand.

"Come sit beside me in front of the tree. We don't have much time. I want you to have these." His angel face filled with excitement, almost as if he'd never given anyone a present.

"Do you celebrate Christmas?"

"Never had anyone I cared to give presents. I meant besides the band or the obligatory business gifts. But for someone special? No."

"But, never anything from you? Your heart?"

"Not 'till tonight, Babe."

"Oh Luka, you're wonderful to me and treat me as if I'm special."

"If you only knew how exceptional you are."

"I wish I had more to give you."

"You have given me more than any man deserves. You've given me my self-respect back and my desire to live instead of making money. I want to build a new life with you. Raise a family with you. You've given me the hope, and you gave me your trust, and that gave me the courage to believe a man like me could be cared for by a lovely lady like you."

He must have seen the crimson shade of red flush her cheeks. No one, even the poetic Kaine had spoken words like those.

"You're not evil Luka. You have done things you're not proud of, we all have."

"You have no idea Babe. And you're wrong. I'm more than acquainted with Lucifer. We are extremely close. Evil is a strong aphrodisiac, and I don't fool myself. I'm as evil as they come."

"But you're not with me."

"My point exactly!"

She dropped her head thinking she'd have to evaluate his comments about being evil against everyone's warnings to her. But not now.

He lifted her chin and placed a well-meaning kiss on her lips to punctuate his words.

"Please, enjoy yourself."

Holly ripped the foil wrappers from the stack of presents with the zest of a nine-year-old. She found books on having a baby and how to raise one, two, and three-year-old children. One on potty training, a fancy baby tub, and rubber water toys. A few blue outfits with sports appliqués sewed on them and bright red and green velvet and silk dresses with tiny lace booties. She unwrapped a football, a baseball glove, a doll, a tea set, and a complete set of small trains, a short stack of fluffy blankets, a bear, giraffe and elephant stuffed animals.

Luka hadn't forgotten anything. The last two presents

were not the usual and produced a sensual smile from her —
a sexy, black, silk lingerie and a jewelry box, revealing a
two-inch diamond bracelet.

"These are for you to wear for me, late into the night
when we make our own baby."

Holly sat on the pile of brightly colored Christmas wrap
with the fruits of Luka's love for her and her growing child
scattered all about her. He would be a wonderful father to
her child and a wonderful husband to her. Her every need
met in and out of the bedroom. Perhaps she should reassess
Luka Hunter and her future.

Luka held her closely, stroking her hair while she kissed
him, her hand roaming his shoulders, hoping to continue,
but he wouldn't.

"I'm close to you Babe, closer than anyone in this
world. I have one last gift." He pulled out an envelope.

Holly opened it to find stock certificates, two shares of
CMT.

"…to secure your future and the babies," he explained.

"Two shares for a future?"

"One day those two shares will be worth more money
than you can ever imagine. Be vigilant with them Holly,
don't be frivolous, be cautious."

Using her name usually meant serious business.

His mood changed with the quickness of lightning.

"We need to catch a plane. CMT wants us on it in less
than an hour. This is the story of my life, always have to be
somewhere else than where I want to be."

Luka pulled away, picked up the paper trail of his love
and stacked his gifts of affection under the tree.

She walked out the door and left untouched, the biggest

present of all — Kaine's.

They drove north over Laurel Canyon to the San Fernando Valley, destination Burbank Airport.

Holly marveled at how much events could change in one day. She'd thought she'd be accustomed to the accelerated pace of her new lifestyle. Luka Hunter, a fast man in a fast lane. She needed to keep up or be left behind. As they drove along, Holly's curiosity got the better of her. "When did you first think I could make money in this unpredictable business?"

"The truth?" He tested, wrapped in mystery.

"Yes, please."

"I'm not certain you want all the entire truth Babe, I'm not at all proud of it."

Chapter Five

THE UGLY TRUTH

olly held her breath. This unpredictable man might
say anything.
"The first time I saw Kaine lay eyes on you."
The impact of the truth hurt worse than expected. She
sighed from the air knocked out of her. That word again!
Every time he said it, it impaled her heart.

"We'd found the right woman."

We? Was he kidding? We? Right woman?

Luka inhaled deeply and slowly exhaled. His eyes slid
quickly to the side to watch her reaction.

"Tell me, Luka." She urged confused.

"This is Christmas day, and I'm not keen on tarnishing
these memories with something I'm not proud of, especially
with what we've done to you, Holly."

We've done! He'd called her by her name meaning this
would be serious.

"I'm not convinced you and I will ever be the same if I
tell you."

"Nothing's going to change what we have Luka?"

"Those words don't make me feel bloody assured ..."

He glanced over at her.

She watched the dark thoughts flash across his face while he decided if he should confess.

"Ticket sales lagged, along with the worse record sales in *Hurrikaine's* history. The music scene changed faster than *Hurrikaine* and the idea of unredeemable outlaws no longer interested the music buying public. We needed to find a way back into the headlines. With safe sex values creeping around the world due to AIDS, we had to create a new era in the bands legend."

"You keep saying we?"

"Well, this isn't public knowledge ... that Kaine and I ... I believe it's a mistake to tell you," he said stalling.

"Tell me!"

"We met in 1986 at Briarwood Castle to start planning this tour. I recall locking ourselves away down in the secret cluster of rooms in the castle, where the recording studio is located. We realized we needed to step up as businessmen and tap the global economy. And instead of riding the current out, we had to crest the wave so-to-speak and create our own headlines.

"It had been easy for too long. Too much money became involved, hundreds of millions of dollars. Hundreds of crew members needed to drag the larger-than-life stage around the world. Kaine and I sat brainstorming."

Luka was right.

Holly wasn't certain she wanted to listen to the minutes of that meeting.

"We need something that will make the world stand up and take notice of us. Two

things sell records in rock 'n' roll. There are sex and drugs, and maybe, love if in a pinch. We need a scandal," Luka said, pacing the cramped room.

"We've had the drug scandals, and enough stories about fucking groupies, socialites, and royalty," Kaine said with disgust.

"That leaves love," Luka said, scrunching his forehead signaling he didn't like that idea either.

Kaine hesitated, not too quick to dismiss the topic. "But it's time for love. We are getting older, and all that settling down rubbish! What if Luka, we found a poor, unsuspecting soul?"

"Yes, a lovely woman that you could find happiness. Not necessarily real love." Luka volunteered.

"Luka, sometimes your English sentiment surprises even me. I can never fall in love. I can't trust any woman anymore. The stakes are too high. All they want is my fucking money, status, or to parade me about. Besides, I love music more that I could ever love anyone woman."

"I see your point. But what if?"

"Yes, I see a plan brewing ... what Luka?"

"It's close. We need a headline that can follow you around the world. We've played on your royal peerage to incite riots here in England. What if we tried to reunite you with your long-lost heritage, a sort of Taming of the

Shrew with a contemporary twist?"

"You 'are' suggesting finding a woman?"

"The right woman, Kaine. She needs to be common, pretty, but not too pretty. Charming, but not too sophisticated, a working woman. Someone the more independent women of today could identify with, the women that buy your records."

"Luka, I think you're bloody on to something. I find this woman and I'll romance her. The rag papers would eat it up for breakfast."

"Exactly. They would follow our every move wondering if she'd become a duchess."

"Promise me, Luka, I don't have to marry this bloody woman. I'm not husband material!"

"We can throw in two or three twists, keep the rags and the world guessing. In the end, of course, after we've cashed our paychecks and with the tour over, you'll have a row. And who will be the wiser?"

"Luka sometimes I believe you're the devil himself instead of his right-hand man."

"That position is reserved for you mate."

"So it would seem."

Luka glanced over to her, but he glanced away as quickly.

She could tell he didn't want to see her reaction as he looked back to the road and before she commented.

"I swear that conversation happened three years ago,

and we've never discussed it since. But the idea had been set in motion. The notion lingered, taking on a life of its own. I soon grew tired of *Hurrikaine's* extended retirement and accepted a position at CMT.

"After a few lucrative business deals, I found no need to return to the *Hurrikaine* machine. However, for the past two years, I did act as a tour consultant to Kaine and Nicky, as they are mainly responsible for putting this tour package together. They'd been good students of mine, watched, and learned from me. They functioned on their own until time to bring in publicity and marketing, and CMT to promote the album, videos, and the documentary.

"Of course, CMT wanted me there due to my long affiliation and knowledge of the band. I reluctantly accepted. First, I owed the band and without them, I wouldn't be where I am."

"And without you, they wouldn't become who they are," she added with a straight tone, protecting herself from Luka noticing her devastation.

"Thanks for your vote of confidence Babe. Second, my contract has not run out yet. But don't get too comfortable. Remember, I'm no angel."

"You expected me that day at the airport?"

"Not you, Babe, but someone. And the moment I saw Kaine laid eyes on you backstage at Wembley Arena I realized she'd arrived."

"I don't remember meeting him backstage. I didn't meet Kaine until the video."

"Oh, remember you had. I'd returned to soften my guilt for leaving you abruptly but found Kaine lurking in the shadows with you, blemishing my good reputation. He called me a tramp. Such rubbish! But, the importance of that meeting? I caught a glimpse of his face, even in the shadows. Kaine, the forever bachelor, was charmed by you, and not with the usual attraction to fuck and abandon. I needed to produce a few more opportune meetings to assure you were indispensable."

Holly fought to keep her voice from trembling, but it didn't stop her lower lip. She'd always forgotten that she'd met Kaine backstage and not at the video shoot. He'd been the mysterious stranger in the shadows, surprised by Luka's restrained behavior toward her.

"You're right Luka. I'm not sure I want to listen."

"Well, luv, I'm in too far to go back. Tell me if you want me to turn this car around when I'm finished." Luka made a quick turn down Mulholland Drive and pulled over into a turnout where a full view of the San Fernando Valley stretched out below their feet.

But Holly didn't notice as pure terror streaking through her veins and the horrible words thundered — words she didn't want to remember.

Luka only does things that are profitable for him.

Don't be fooled by Luka.

Luka's capable of anything.

Aptly capable of turning her entire world upside down, and she couldn't take it again.

Luka turned the car engine off, and he stared straight ahead.

"I thought if Kaine would transfer the chemistry between him and you in those few moments, onto video tape, but most importantly, if you responded like you looked … well, that became the origin of the video shoot at the Hard

Rock. I needed to get you written in straightaway, and from then on, THE project started to jell."

"You're saying I became THE project."

Would the twisting knots in her stomach ever stop?

"Sooo, the next morning when you came to my hotel, it's exactly as I'd suspected, it wasn't an audition. I'd already secured the job. You arrived to prime me. To teach me to take directions and sexually respond to Kaine the way he wanted. To have me hot and sexually charged and melt under Kaine's reputed charms."

"Something like that — though I've never met the woman that hasn't fallen for Kaine."

What an arrogant remark!

Overcome with shock that Luka the nerve to say that nonchalantly, Holly wanted to laugh and smash his face at the same time.

"Babe, I felt uncomfortable throwing you to the devil due to the ingenious way you'd responded to me. Well, let's say your pure heart touched the last thread of decency in me.

"I'm not what you think Holly. I'm not a nice chap, I never have been. And neither is Kaine. But, he may have forgotten our conversation in the castle. I think he saw you with me and the old competition flared — as I originally hoped. But to his credit, after three years to clean up, and do a bit of soul-searching, well, the time had mellowed him. The old bastard seemed 'ready and willing' to fall in love, except it turned out to be with you."

Holly sat stunned and embarrassed by Luka's confession and asked. "And you?"

"I hope you can forgive this, but from the first day, you

were the sacrificial lamb. I didn't deserve a lovely lady like you, but neither did Kaine, however, if he wanted you, he could have you. Or, as I thought then. I started to notice your differences from other women. The way you looked at me — with such innocence without knowledge of my nefarious dealings. That I could accomplish the impossible with you, Babe.

"It's a wonderful feeling to be cared for ... for being me. One I never thought I'd ever experience again. You had made the impossible happen. You Babe, with your warmth and kisses and willingness to give to me, convinced me that even I had a chance at love again, possibly a future."

Holly didn't want to listen to his words of love — not mixed with the ugly truth and deceit.

"If I'm correct, you're responsible for my part of the video shoot?"

"Spot on, Babe."

"Kaine told me that in London, but I didn't understand your influence."

"Sometimes, I amaze myself." He chuckled and nodded his head.

Luka Hunter, more powerful and dangerous than she'd ever believed possible. He alone played master puppeteer, changing the entire course of her future. She found it difficult to identify the barrage of upsetting and discouraging emotions that currently fought for her immediate attention. She took a breath, promising herself to listen before she got out of the car and started walking.

"I don't think anyone at that stage of the project comprehended how the CMT contest winner would put *Hurrikaine* back in the headlines. I pushed, use new clout I recently acquired."

Yes, she thought, *like owning shares of the company.*

"I convinced Michael, and Clive at CMT-UK, to substitute you in the Hard Rock shot instead of Germany's leading model and bloody pissed her off badly. She complained loudly about being bumped, especially in her estimation by an unknown."

"You're speaking of Claudine Michaels. That's why you accommodated to her?"

"Correct, left with the dirty job of easing her ruffled feathers."

"An overnighter you'd called her."

"And that's when you started, luv."

"Me?"

"Let's say, Kaine's evaluation of me with women is accurate."

"You mean when he called you a tramp."

"I've told you, women come easily to me. But that night was different. You'd left the engagement party with Kaine, and I couldn't do my job and go boff Claudine — something or someone changed me. You. And my involvement increased the stakes, especially with Kaine."

"Am I part of your job?" Holly could barely keep her tears at bay. But she would not let this bastard have the satisfaction of making her cry again.

Luka's facial expression said don't go there.

He took off his hat and ran his fingers through his gorgeous hair.

"You're bloody right. I shouldn't tell you this. It's not going to help anyone. If anything, I may destroy the best thing that ever happened to me."

His honest words touched her heart. She softened. Perhaps being Luka Hunter was difficult, and someone needed to give him a chance. One chance!

"No, Luka. You'll not run this time. You've been running for long enough. Give me the courtesy of the truth. I might surprise you."

"You already have, Holly."

Luka glanced down at the clock in the car.

"We've got to hurry to make the plane."

"Luka don't do this. I need the rest of the story to decide *if* I will get on that plane."

STAY WITH ME TONIGHT

L uka started the car and flipped his gorgeous hair behind his shoulder, but his angel face seemed tarnished. And Holly started to understand what it took to be Luka Hunter and take *Hurrikaine* to the top of the world.

It took cunning, daring, and most of all, no conscience to become Luka Hunter, a deceitful, and manipulative man — Tessa's assessment apparently spot on — *Luka's quite capable of anything.*

He drove faster.

Holly feared his injurious confessions would run them off the mountain.

"I was confident," he said easily, "just a matter of time, and you would become a household name. Especially after a bit of research and learned of your notoriety being Holly Hill from the Collins, murder trial. My instincts are never wrong."

"You were aware of who I am, essentially from the start?"

He nodded yes and conceded.

"Of course. When you left with Kaine after the Hard Rock, I sent a photographer to follow you. Kaine would eventually respond to your beauty, and I wanted it captured on film.

"Kaine played his part perfectly, especially kissing you in front of England's most recognizable icon, Buckingham Palace. I think I'm quoted in the paper as 'a well-meaning fan took the picture'? Twenty-four hours later all of England wanted details about Kaine's mystery lady."

"That's why you sent me with Kaine after the video shoot?"

Holly remembered asking Kaine about the man following them. Kaine thought security, apparently, he didn't know what Luka planned then either.

"Exactly! Also, why I planted the idea of you being his girlfriend early on, to add stability to the story and lock you in for the duration of the week to speed up the romance. He agreed to the idea the next morning when I told him on the phone. Remember when I called about the castle shoot. I needed to get him on board with the idea by testing the water, telling him about the newspaper article naming you as his girlfriend. If you remember, he didn't show any signs of not wanting that. The old sod would have told me to 'kill the rag.' Our code words for not on board, but he agreed. And that's when events started to change faster."

"This is not making me comfortable, Luka."

"It will get much worse before then, Babe."

"Sounds like London became one big publicity stunt," she jeered.

"I couldn't have orchestrated a publicity stunt as easy as you and Kaine made it. Your affair fell into my lap and then rolled onto the headlines. Your romance moved quickly. It had a life of its own, and I did my best to keep one step ahead of the landfall about to hit *Hurrikaine.*"

"You mean?" He had her.

"Yes, the Hard Rock rushes. You're one of the lucky ones the camera loves, and you're intelligent, to be involved with the Collins murder trial. And I should add, to have the courage to walk into what waited for you as Kaine Walker's girlfriend and not turn tail and run. You proved me right. It would take someone, not of our decadent world, but familiar with controversy and headlines, to come in and brazenly tamper with the infamous *Hurrikaine.*"

Brazen. Not a term she would ever use to define herself.

"Especially, to tamper with Kaine and ME, we are notorious — our sexual depravity and prowess are well publicized. To all but you, luv."

"Everything you did, a conniving and deceitful game," she affirmed, wishing her next breath would make her vanish. Let her die a quiet death without the details that London served as a hoax and that this time with Luka nothing more than a strategy, an ugly, devious, and heartless scheme.

"Maybe once, but not for long. The chain of events changed too quickly straightaway due to you."

"Me? I never stood a chance with the two of you." She capitulated, her voice laced with disgust.

"Oh, but you did. And continue do...."

She half smiled not knowing why while the rush of demoralizing emotions ran too fast and was too confusing to sort through quickly at the moment.

Luka glanced over at her.

She'd never seen him worried.

"You acted different from the start, unpredictable. I think I loved you from the first moment I saw you. Your sweetness made me remember I'm a man first, and that music and the next deal don't have to be my whole bloody life. I started to change, and then other things changed, like my gratitude that with you, I could have a real life. But by then I had pushed you into the headlines with Kaine. And I selfishly wanted you back. I didn't want the game. I didn't want the headlines. I didn't want the fucking money. I wanted you.

"That realization arrived when you stood in the dressing room in Briarwood Castle turning for me. I watched you wanting to please me, loving your beautiful face, your innocence, and sweetness, but too late, overnight you'd become Kaine's girlfriend.

"That's when I decided to do everything possible to keep you in my life until you wanted one with me, and that day is today. I want you on that plane with me."

Getting on planes did seem to define her. Did she know what she wanted anymore? Luka's staggering confession scared her too, along with his sovereign power.

"I want to be with you, Luka, but there's more. You want me to get on that plane. Well, I must trust you. And, you must trust me. Can you trust me enough to tell me everything? Let me make up my mind knowing all the facts?"

"I don't tell secrets, Holly. That's what you want from me."

"Yes, I need answers, that this relationship is real, not artificial feelings meant to deceive the public with an elaborate hoax. A selfish game played out by two internationally famous and extremely wealthy men so board, they sat and mastermind a devious scheme, to dupe the world out of billions of dollars. Luka, I need to trust that you're real."

Luka pulled up to the airport parking. He threw her a cautious glance.

"I'll tell you on the plane."

He reached out and ran his fingers through her hair and on around to hold her head. He pulled her face to him, placing her a mint-scented breath away from kissing her.

"Do you want me?" His eyes are filled with worry.

Was his revelation true?

Or, the confession real?

Holly remained close but didn't kiss him, trying to tell him that to that point he hadn't frightened her enough to leave. Even though every instinct inside her screamed, RUN!!!

Her intuition was always on the money about him. To run as fast and as far from Luka Hunter as she possibly could.

But there was nowhere to run.

Too late.

She'd learned the dreadful truth after signing the six-month contract with him and CMT. She'd done everything possible to get him into her bed. Well, he slept there nightly. And he'd explained how she belonged to him. How could she cross him and not fear his retaliation from his powerful connections?

No, she'd made this bed and put him in it with her — a bed where he wanted to give her his strange love that might break her.

No, for the time being, she had to join in the game, no longer a pawn, but a player — though out of her league, but she'd learn fast.

Luka had been correct — evil was a powerful aphrodisiac.

They boarded the CMT jet and settled in the plush swivel chairs. Refreshments were served and after a few instructions to the attendants were left alone.

Holly sat beside Luka.

He lifted her hand and gently draped it across his and admitted. "I've dreaded this moment since Briarwood — the moment I would tell you the bloody ugly truth about this nasty business."

"I've come this far Luka. Tell me. Tell me what you keep hidden. Tell me everything."

"Sex. That became the key because we're in the business of selling love songs. As the number one reigning bachelor and the Duke of Dunnehill, it would be sensational headlines for him to fall in love and take a bride, a duchess — too bloody difficult to resist. I could sit back and let nature take its course and let the rags run the headlines free of charge and sell more records.

"I fed the love story to the paparazzi and Fleet Street, and ticket sales went through the roof. Not to mention setting new record sales and the *Hurrikaine* song catalog got a hefty boost too. CMT's exclusive documentary of *Hurrikaine's Lost Dreams ... Lost Illusions* world tour would bring in old and new viewers, not to mention the added sales from the video."

Holly should have been astonished, but she sat

motionless, holding her rage intact. "What made you think it would work?"

"Please, Babe. Don't take offense to how this will sound, but you're the commoner, our dream come true ... even better, an American. That insured international interest. And to enter a contest and win a chap like Kaine, a descendant of royal lineage, rich and internationally famous, would make extraordinary headlines. It would work for you and Kaine. He wanted you, who wouldn't, Babe.

"But Kaine surprised me. I'd never seen him react to any woman as he did to you. He'd put you first over his usual selfish wants and needs, brushed off his best manners and made plans for a future with you. He showed up all gentlemen, something I'd never seen in him. He'd changed, no longer the roguish bastard, and selfish, spoiled rock star we knew him to be.

"Something important happened and everyone, in and around the *Hurrikaine* machine, watched something extraordinary happen. Especially Rah, sorry, Kaine's longtime companion, isn't that's how I phrased it?"

She'd never forget that bitch, Sarah Cromwell. Trapped with her down in that dark corridor at Friar Manor where Sarah beat the shit out of her and laid the cold gun muzzle against her cheek.

Never would she forget how Sarah threatened to shoot her in the head with Kaine's gun and then frame him for the murder. Yes, one day she would get even with Sarah Cromwell.

What she succinctly stated, "That bitch?"

"Yes. That bitch and a lot more, it would seem by your story of what happened in the corridor at Friar Manor."

"Well, you're a master at manipulating the headlines. In or out of the papers. Especially, keeping Friar Manor out of the papers." Holly complemented, wondering if he'd noticed the sarcasm.

"It's too easy sometimes. I fed the media your hot, whirlwind romance. Nothing could stop the "Now That I've Found You" video from being a smash hit, and to capture Kaine falling in love, for the entire world to see, brilliant! The world loves to be a voyeur into the lives of the rich and famous. And how lucky can a chap get? Kaine had up and written "Now That I've Found You" and you walked in the bloody door?

"You do see I only kept up feeding photos and news briefs on the celestial love affair. The rest you and Kaine supplied quite naturally."

"Luka, what do I say? I see why you said at the castle that I had to go to him because I couldn't fuck-up the publicity. Because then I'd never become the Heart of the *Hurrikaine.*"

"Catchy title. I had fed the sound bite to Solange at the castle, and she unknowingly delivered the headline perfectly."

"Oh Luka, how could you?"

"I told you music's an ugly business."

"But," she paused and sighed. "Luka.... Was anything real?"

"Your love for Kaine, that's the single reason it all worked. What got in the way of Kaine's love for you became the drugs. And, of course, his legion of devils waiting to be unleashed. I'm not positive what that's all about, I assumed the pressure was building, and he wanted to be numb to everything but you. But drugs aren't discriminatory.

"I agree with your analysis of Kaine's behavior at Friar Manor. The alcohol and drugs pushed Kaine's buttons causing him to break. It surprised me how quickly he fell apart. I'd figured we'd have the European Tour sewn up before anyone would have to factor into the equation Kaine's escalating drug abuse. But, by then, I'd be back in L.A., at CMT, and he'd become someone else's fucking problem for a change."

"Luka, you make the business sound cold, and heartless."

"It is! Selling music is a cruel, cold multi-billion dollar business. The weak are always crushed and bodies left in the wake like road kill.

"But that's where my problems started. Kaine's dark side surfaced quickly. Remember, your story of how roughly he treated you after the sound check. Well, that's when I worried about you being in over your head.

"That day I needed to acknowledge how important you became to me. The innocence in the arms of a drug driven rock star gone mental, spoon-fed to him by me no less! Imagine my dilemma?

"I handed the woman I desired over to the volatile Kaine. The one way I could keep you safe was to keep you high profile. Hence, sensational stories about the Heart of the *Hurrikaine*. I had to keep the best drugs coming to control Kaine even if it didn't look like it. But I want you to know, I was never, ever, too far away."

"But that's not true Luka … down in the dark corridor with Kaine raving at me like a madman due to kissing you, I was all alone."

"I'm sorry Babe. And I'll never forgive myself. I will spend the rest of my life trying to make that up to you. Rah sent me on a wild-goose chase looking for lost equipment, I had no idea Kaine saw me kissing you. Before I could figure out what happened, Rah told me he drug you somewhere.

"I arrived from another direction and not near enough to see which way he'd taken you. The Manor was a big place, and unfortunately, he'd finished with you before I found you lying ..." Luka swallowed unable to finish his sentence. The hatred flared hot in his eyes, it shined brightly.

A pinch of sorrow rumbled through her thoughts for Kaine if Luka ever looked at him again with those eyes.

"Luka, you have the facts, Sarah hurt me, not Kaine." She offered with more sympathy that she wanted.

It had been her down in the fucking corridor, not Luka, but she did understand his fear for her. "I count myself lucky you found me and covered the paper trail with enough money to conceal how badly she beat me. What an awful position to be."

"You'll never know! Because I believed, Kaine wounded you badly. It was a good thing I didn't carry my gun that night, or I wouldn't be here with you. It was later your faint recollections suspected her. I didn't have any proof until you confirmed it the other night. As a side note Babe, I will take care of Rah for what she did to you.

"When we left Friar Manor, I couldn't take you to hospital. My own sensational story prevented you from getting the best help money could buy. With the bands private surgeon too far from Friar Manor in London, I couldn't risk a leak of that magnitude to the press. I couldn't call in the authorities and have Kaine cautioned, as I first thought, as he should have been. But Kaine hadn't physically attacked you. And as out of line as you started he was apart from losing his temper, and spewing foul words, he hadn't truly harmed you.

"You and I went to the other surgeon and made do. Cost me hundreds of pounds to keep him quiet, little enough, because millions of dollars rested on the success of the tour which would generate more money for CMT."

More money for you, she thought.

You own so much stock in CMT, Luka.

Why won't you tell me?

Holly sat quietly, pressed against the back of the seat, amazed at how out of touch with reality she'd been in London, not to mention the past four months. How perfectly orchestrated, her life had been.

Hadn't Luka told Michael to give her back pay for London? Now she understood why she'd been on the payroll, she'd been executing her job since day one. And what a great job she'd done for CMT!

Indeed, she'd played her role as seductress flawlessly, but then she'd been directed perfectly by the master — Luka Hunter. This devilishly handsome man that manipulated and controlled people with no conscience.

"Many times I hated myself and glad you didn't fancy me. I'd done deplorable things, and to you. I thought that when you went home to L.A., you would be free of us. None of us at the core of the *Hurrikaine* machine is any good, Holly. You didn't deserve anything that happened to you. Fuck Babe, that became the second worst night of my life."

"Second? Second worse, when was the first?"

His eyes became guarded. Another secret he wasn't ready to share.

"I have a publicity nightmare. You're telling me you hate rock 'n' roll, and the Heart of the *Hurrikaine* never wants to lay eyes on Kaine again. Bloody Hell! I understand, but the video rushed to air. You needed to be reunited with Kaine and have time to heal, except, time ran out. Fuck, Babe, it was a bloody nightmare for all concerned."

"But more for you. You had Kaine, CMT, and me to appease. And you couldn't please us all, could you, Luka? You lost control, and you hate that most of all, don't you, Luka?"

She confirmed her disgust by shaking her head as if in disbelief.

What a selfish bastard you are as everyone said.

He nodded his head in agreement.

"Kaine's wounded, too much drink, doing more drugs, tearing up the hotel room as a one hit touring band. He loathed himself. But in the end, things worked out. I stayed close to you. I thought everything would get better. I'd had it with Kaine. You would go to L.A., and I would be in L.A. A couple of days after Paris, the *Hurrikaine* video would be completed, and my affiliation with *Hurrikaine* finished forever. *Hurrikaine* would be behind us. You and I could start to build a future."

All along, he'd been far ahead of her. She'd never had a chance to make any real decisions for herself. They'd all been born out of the choices Luka presented her. And he'd had all the scenarios covered in case, as he did currently.

What she offered.

"I'm sorry, Luka. These past months have been a living hell for you and me. We've had enough pain. Time we all healed. Put the ugly scenarios in the past and look forward."

Luka gazed at her guardedly as if she was testing him, and then as if he'd never heard her words started to point out.

"No one knows better than I do about what you were up against, Babe. Kaine's an amazingly charismatic man, impossible to know, impossible to forget. I understand. I'm the one who created his press bio, and the one that always had to comfort all of his discards, to protect the band from lawsuits when he ruthlessly tossed women aside. Part of his old rock star image as a confirmed womanizer.

"But it's not a contrived image.

"He's a cold-hearted, cruel bastard.

"Something hidden inside Kaine made him hate women. I'm not clear if it goes back to his mother dying unexpectedly, or how at an early age, women threw themselves at him, and I don't bloody care.

"I didn't want you to become another statistic of Kaine's. Many Babe, too many have and I wanted to spare you."

She thought Kaine could certainly argue the same case about Luka, having women throw themselves at him and then heartlessly abandoning them. And here she was a possible statistic for either man.

"But after he recorded your song "Cold Without You" in Paris, I realized the old Kaine had indeed grown up and became a man committed and in love with you. Also, that if Kaine survived the drug abuse, he wouldn't give you up, and he'd fight to win you back.

"I went to him the last morning in London and pleaded for him to let you go, to let me give you a good life. That's when the fight broke out at his hotel.

"I knew then, he loved you, for him to agree, finally, to let me take you with me. But Babe, understand, I had to get you away from Kaine for good."

Chapter Seven

THE KING OF HOLLYWOOD

K *aine agreed to let me take you....*
No decision left to her.
Everything, easy for Luka.

She'd been given to him, his for the taking.

"I wasn't without means," he stated interrupting her thoughts.

Holly gave up trying to comment. Each revelation became more horrifying than the last. Nothing in London was it seemed and none of the past four months real. All a horribly fabricated plan, designed to capture the headlines to make money. This landfall of the *Hurrikaine* left many lives destroyed. More dreams shattered for money — lots of money, billions of dollars.

She looked at Luka wondering who he was.

Did human blood flow in his veins?

Did a heart beat under his scrumptious chest?

Was he a man?

A real flesh and blood man?

Luka continued, breaking into her stunned presence.

"I insisted Michael hire you for the job of the hostess on

the new interview show. I had the last piece in place. I can maneuver Michael to do anything I want."

"How Luka, how influential are you that you gave me my own show?" Maybe this the time he would confess? But the apprehension washed over her leaving her uncertain she was ready for the truth.

"Remember the last night in Sheridan? One of the men is a solicitor. Can you keep a secret?"

"I'll do my best."

This was it!

"Not good enough. You can't tell anyone."

"Okay. Trust me."

"I'm trying. Would you take a blood oath to never tell?"

She understood what he asked. Would she pledge her whole life to keep the blood oath as she did long ago in her childhood? Luka believed that she would never break the blood oath, not for anyone.

"Yes," she said, raising her eyes to meet his. She knew exactly what to do. She'd sign the damn blood pact with the Devil.

"Well, then. I'll tell you. Remember the meeting in the den?"

"Yes."

"Those men that gathered that last night are investors."

"Yes, go on, Luka?"

He would tell her.

He did trust her.

There wasn't a guarantee she should be glad or not? For Luka to trust her meant she would never be free of him. They would go on forever, side-by-side. He wasn't the man she wanted to share the rest of her life with, or for that matter, did she ever have a choice?

Whatever Luka wants, Luka gets. And that's you.

Everyone in the Hurrikaine camp kept repeating that mantra to her.

"We closed the deal for music's future. As my financial backers, I bought stock in CMT. I own the controlling stock, fifty-one percent. The problem, Kaine bought the other forty-nine percent of CMT out from under me. He thought I'd never find out he bought them. But I did while in San Francisco.

"The virus, bloody lie. He wasn't ill at the castle, or on the tour. That stupid cover story was planted to hide his secret negotiations, putting together a secret coup to own CMT outright. Or, so he thought. The funny thing is — *he* doesn't realize I own the other fifty-one percent. Imagine his surprise when he learns that I will always own him?"

Holly flashed back to Luka's words when he gave her the stock as a gift.

Someday those two stocks shares will be worth more money than you can ever imagine.

Holly quickly calculated the math. She owned two shares, which left Luka with forty-nine percent, meaning when they married, together they owned controlling interest in CMT. That explained why he responded as he did when she'd dared to ask him what would happen if she said no to his next marriage proposal.

But you won't will you.

He had it all figured out.

"You?"

She tried to sound surprised, and that was true, Kaine

owned the other half! And she held the controlling stock? The payoff for her silence, imagine the possibilities? She remembered the night in Sheridan, a seemingly happy family gathering, all a staged front for an international music coup with Luka as the ringleader. He *was* capable of anything. But as an astute businessman, she'd known that since the night in Sheridan. She wasn't as blasé as she appeared.

However, the real news alert, Kaine's illness in Europe, a cover for another heinous deception. She'd worried that his condition happened due to her behavior. She'd nothing to do with it. Oh, of course, he'd been depressed about their break-up, performing *My Lady*, and recording, but he hadn't fallen apart as suggested. And those revelations lent themselves to more questions.

Why had the Ghost of Briarwood surfaced since there had been no therapy as Emily said? And why would Emily lie to her all this time? But she didn't have the time to digest those points.

Luka continued to share. And every word he spoke became extremely important — maybe her entire future depending on them.

"Michael is always keen to do anything to keep me happy for two reasons. One, because he wanted to remain CEO of both CMT–UK and CMT–USA, and two, he didn't want to lose me as the controlling investor."

Holly sighed and added as if defeated.

"Even willing to hire an unknown, you created, but then took a fancy to and gave her a national T.V. show?"

"I wouldn't characterize it that way. The woman had to be personable, professional, intelligent, photogenic, and lastly able to carry the responsibilities of a national show. Even I couldn't give you all that. You supplied that."

"Why Luka? Why do you walk about CMT like a hired hand? Like Lilly asked you in London why are you in the trenches getting your hands dirty?"

"Think about what you've said. I move about freely. If anyone outside a small privy of colleagues realized my position, I would become Kaine, a prisoner of my own creation. It's bloody bad enough being labeled as Kaine's personal manager. Enough of my freedom has been stolen from me, especially my trust in humanity. Money changes people, and big money creates greedy, corrupt, and dangerous people in my humble experience."

"Even you?" She asked quietly.

"Especially me. You have been privy to my dealings with unimaginable high sums of money. I don't want anyone to have the secret information of who holds fifty-one percent. Excuse me forty-nine since I gave you two percent — but a game-changing percentage. My shares are hidden under enough paper, to keep a lot of people digging for years to connect it to me. In the meantime, I have the money and the power to make or break CMT, which, by the way, includes *Hurrikaine*. And there's one other crucial reason."

"Tessa?"

"That's why you're my lady. You keep up, and as I said, the skies not the limit Babe, small dreams can keep you down, and if you don't dream big enough, you'll be squashed."

He'd called her My Lady. Taking over again. She hid her annoyance and questioned him.

"You truly believe I can make it in this cut-throat

business?"

"You already have a following, and the camera loves you. You play guitar, giving us an unusual hook for the shows closing. Yes, you can make it, or I never would have given it to you."

She noticed his emphasis, the implied *us*.

… I never would have given it to you.

"You have. And Frank? He didn't recommend me?"

"No. But oddly enough, he saw the same potential I did. He's an old timer, and Michael would have listened to him even if I hadn't stepped in with my suggestion. You're perfect, made for the show. He merely confirmed my original evaluation of you. We're not wrong. Miss Hill, you're certain to become an international hit. With Kaine behind us, and with me to guide your career, only your imagination is the limit. We can be together, take on the world, and succeed until you tire of me. I'm hoping that takes a long, long time."

Welcome to another Luka Hunter Production.

Since Kaine's career ended, he'd replaced him with her. He'd made *Hurrikaine* and Kaine worldwide stars. And with his record of accomplishments, that was his plan for her.

Holly sat back shell-shocked from Luka's explosive bombs. All the happenings behind the scenes had been orchestrated by Luka while she meandered blindly through her fairy tale affair playing her part as directed with Kaine. How terribly naive she'd been, all the unnecessary worry, the ridiculous mind games with herself about whether she should choose Kaine or Luka.

It never mattered.

Luka already decided.

Kaine's words came blasted back powerfully because this time, they described her current situation.

What I think is of little use, I am to sell tickets and records. He is my personal manager/producer.

What would have happened to her if there had not been a Luka Hunter?

Simple, she'd be with Kaine, married and happy. Not out signing contracts and making blood pacts with the devil. And Luka wouldn't have tormented Kaine.

Her body jerked involuntarily because her heart splintered into a thousand pieces. Her hand went protectively to the sacred space where she carried the heir apparent. But Luka deviated from the original plan, changing everything and fallen into a strange love with her and he wanted Kaine's baby. But if she'd never told anyone that the child belonged to Kaine's, then there would be no inheritance, no royal title. Emily, at least, made that clear.

Emily straightened her out. Her child deserved to have the right of refusal. Not be dictated by Luka and alter her child's future forever. Well, maybe he'd been able to manipulate everyone, thus far, but it would stop today, she had her child's future to plan. Of course, Luka stayed miles ahead of her. He'd known what her marrying him would do to Kaine's heir apparent.

Holly sat emotionally wounded, her faith in Luka dying a slow, torturous death. She looked at him and drank in his handsome face, the face of a gorgeous angel.

And she answered him from behind a false face she created.

"I like the idea of being with you for a very, very long time."

She covered his leather-gloved hand with hers and squeezed him meaningfully. For the time being, he became her future whether she wanted him or not. She wasn't afraid of him, but she understood she should be.

Moreover, she'd already activated her better sense not to cross him. She was up to speed, starting to think about how to create her own future, but most importantly, her child's future.

Holly smiled and with that admission, something snapped inside her. She'd been taught by the best, the master manipulator and she'd learned fast.

Things were about to change.

Three would play this game.

She was finally a player.

The Unholy Trinity in full swing.

"How did I get so lucky?" She mockingly added.

Chapter Eight

STRANGE WAY

Too much information to process! Holly wanted to cover her ears and block out every atrocious word of Luka's monstrous admission. Everyone had been right. He was exactly the monster they'd all believed him to be.

"Has my ugly confession changed your feelings toward me?"

Luka asked quietly as if her answer meant something to him. He'd been watching her, his eyes narrowed, trying to read her.

Apparently, she was doing well, disguising her revulsion, and presenting the new face, the facade that said 'I will forsake Kaine and love you forever.'

"Yes, many things have changed between us. My feelings are different. I have a deeper respect for your cunning business talent. And knowing you're in control at CMT has its benefits. About Kaine and I? I'm understandably upset, of course, since I know the facts of London. And I feel confused when I think of my future, *our* future. Give me a little time to adjust to this new Luka

Hunter, global entrepreneur."

"It's yours, a small penance to pay for what I've done to you. We do have the gift of time, Babe."

Did they? Kaine was coming for her in six days. That was all she had to endure. Six long, torturous days. And she understood why Kaine told her he'd done terrible things he never wanted her to learn. Well, she knew some of them. And for once, she did have a choice, and she'd made it. For the moment, she knew whom she would choose. Fight for! For the time being, she knew her part, and she knew how to play her part well.

The flight to Tucson was eerie. She stared out the window doing a bit of math trying to figure out how many hours she would have to endure Luka. By her calculations, she'd have to convince Luka of her sincerity for two days. The schedule was tight, there wasn't much left of today and then tomorrow was the shoot with Jaden, then the *Bon Jour* concert tomorrow night.

She wasn't clear if they were returning to L.A., tomorrow night or the following morning.

At most, it was forty–eight hours with Luka. She could do what was necessary to him for that amount of time if it meant that Kaine and her baby would remain safe.

Once in L.A., she'd pretend to be too busy with all the pre-wedding events. That should keep Luka from hanging around her until Kaine arrived.

For the present, she had a plan and decided to take what came. Try to enjoy all of what Luka had to offer because one thing she believed was, he loved her. Not necessarily, the kind of love she wanted, but his loving her meant for the time being he wouldn't harm her. But joining the party in progress meant taking what she wanted from him and then leave in six days with Kaine.

Yes, her tutelage was from a master Svengali. Luka's malicious intent to control all of her and Kaine, and really anyone he was in contact with, was always smooth. From servers breaking their backs to get his every need met, to CEOs like Michael giving her a show to please him. His talent to persuade was masked by his use of kindness and concern. Those were his master tools with her. The proof was the fact that he owned her as her producer and manager. He really dominated any and all decisions for or about her. But knowing this did give her an edge, albeit tiny. She was a new graduate and a full-fledged active member in the exclusive Unholy Trinity — Luka, Kaine and herself. She wasn't positive that after landfall which would be left standing.

It was the two of them and the pilot. It was silent. It was unnerving because Luka had asked the crew to leave the plane in L.A. after they'd attended to their needs. She understood why. The CMT information was too hot to trust someone overhearing.

Her head spun finding it difficult to believe anything Luka said. Even her affair with Kaine had been a set-up. Forty-nine percent of CMT was Luka's. Forty-nine percent belonged to Kaine. And she and the baby held the all-important two percent!

Why would Luka put her in this position?

Oh, she'd caught up, all right!

Holly knew the kill would be sweeter when she threw in her two percent to join with Luka. Then, of course, Luka would be controlling Kaine. 'Own him,' he'd said, once again along with the multi-billion dollar empire.

She looked at him again with awe.

Who the fuck was Luka Hunter?

A short time later, while practicing on Slick, she watched Luka, wondering where her good sense had been these past months.

Some time later, she sat the gift from Kaine down on the plush sofa, walked over to Luka, who busied himself with a stack of production sheets. She leaned over his shoulder as he sipped a mineral water. The hum of the engines soothed her frayed nerves after his life-shattering bombs.

She bent closer to his ear hidden behind his long hair and remarked, "You know if I weren't blown away from your revelations, I'd join the mile high club with you."

Luka looked up at her.

She hated to admit that he did look adorable, yet distinguished with his reading spectacles perched on the edge of his nose.

He looked up at her with his eyebrows arched.

"I can top that. If I wasn't exhausted, I'd of had you already. We are a pair."

They broke into a much-needed laugh seemingly happy to have found each other.

Or, as she wanted him to believe.

Holly stood behind his chair massaging his shoulders thinking aloud.

"I'm pleased that we really have a relationship based on more than sex. As you said, I realize you're my whole life. You're my manager, producer, and lover, soon to be the father of my child, and one day my husband. You have all of me. I have no choices left to make."

He looked up and smiled as if to confirm her words.

"Brilliant! You've decided to allow me to father your baby ... our baby."

Finally, she had him right where she wanted him. There was one problem left to work out, how to protect Kaine, the baby and herself from both Luka and Sarah?

"I think next year will be a bright year for you and me," she predicted.

"Well, our relationship may not be based solely on sex, but if we bloody keep on like last night, I won't see the New Year," Luka teased.

"Don't say that! Don't even joke! What would I do without you?"

He pulled the glasses from the edge of his nose, turned and looked straight into her eyes and stated.

"You would go with Kaine when he comes for you," his tone cold and matter-of-factly.

He was correct, but she remarked.

"Why would you say something as horrible as that?"

"You think Kaine is that horrible?"

She didn't answer.

"I thought naught. But it's bloody simple, really. Kaine's in love with you, and he's stubborn, and like me is willing to wait. For the moment, the tables have turned, and he is waiting for me to drop the ball." He placed his warm, heavy hand over hers. "You do realize he's coming for you?"

Holly started to tremble, but whether it was due to dread or excitement, she couldn't distinguish.

"Does that bloody well bother you knowing how strong Kaine's feelings are for you? Especially since he doesn't know you're carrying his child."

Holly squeezed Luka's fingers knowing it was difficult for him to ask her. But she needed to be careful with her answer.

"No. No, it doesn't. I'll always have a place in my heart for Kaine. I'll always love him. He was my second lover and has become the father of my child. I owe."

"Second lover?" Luka's tone changed dramatically.

Holly swallowed a smile.

"Yes, second. Remember, my husband Jon was my first lover? I thought I told you the entire tragic story in London."

"You did, that Jon was killed on your wedding night. I do remember. I guess I forgot. I'm sorry, Babe. I hope I didn't upset or scare you last night?"

"Did I look scared?"

"Well, no. I confess with all the confusion, I've assumed you'd been intimate with Brett. I forgot you told me in London you'd been with two men, Jon, and Kaine. Somehow, I assumed others had made their way to you. You're irresistible Babe, and well, let's say loving."

"I'm surprised. Aren't all women attracted to you like the one in San Francisco, loving?"

"No. Other women? Hell no! With them, it's plain sex, not love. There is no loving or tenderness with them. The women I'm exposed to are about performance. And I'm sorry that's what I thought was your experience. I understand, it's your innocence and interest to please me and the wonderment of what pleasure with me can be. What will it special make loving to you is knowing you come to me without prior carnal knowledge of a lot of what I have shared with you. And Babe, that makes the loving even sweeter. I know that with you, the loving, the tenderness all comes from you wanting to share your desire to please me, and for us to enjoy loving each other." Luka sat back. He looked at Holly, giving her a look of 'should I tell you this'.

"The women I'm exposed to are greatly experienced in everything but loving me. They are the opposite of you. Their goal is to impress me with their carnal knowledge because they believe that's what I expect.

"They pursue me. It's been a long time since I have had to put any energy into the chase. But with you, it's different.

"You have drawn me out, brought out the man in me since those first moments in Chelsea where I rushed to rescue you from the on-coming traffic.

"You need me, but you wait for me to come to you.

"You don't question me, or demand details of my time when I'm not with you.

"And that is vastly different from my usual experiences with women. Look at Kaine. He came after you, not the other way around, Babe. That must have blown his mind too. Especially, when you didn't capitulate. He's never experienced that either.

"When I realized I had to back off and wait for you to decide between us ... well, I'll tell you this. I've never waited for any woman in my life. But you have an innocence about you that allow a man to want to be with you. And I find that quality to be loving."

"Loving means naïve — again."

"Not necessary."

"It sounds like it! Jon didn't have experience with techniques like you, he used a young man's love — his heart. The other knowledge I brought to you was from what Kaine taught me, but that was a few days of experiences. I took the experiences of heart, gave it to Kaine, and was willing to love him anyway he wanted. But you're correct. I arrived with little carnal knowledge. I couldn't foresee, much less dream of the multitude of techniques involved with loving that has come to me from both of you. You must realize that due to the ways you love me, the results are these incredibly hot, lusty feelings for you because no one else can."

Luka started to speak.

She kissed him quickly, then slowly and then dropped into his magic as if the kiss was endless. It was difficult to open her glazed eyes when she'd finished because kissing evil was an unusual aphrodisiac.

"It's all right, truly. Kaine believed the same as you. He was equally surprised, but even more with the fact that you hadn't slept with me. That was when he knew you were in deeper than even you knew.

"His initial reaction to me was to back off too, and he treated me like a delicate virgin that needed gentle handling. Always concerned if he'd offended or frightened me. But not last night with you.

"You didn't treat me as virginal or a bit naïve, needing to be taught. But you both wanted to keep me and my carnal experiences all to yourselves.

"I guess, all in all, I've really put one over on you two sophisticated men of the world. Like me, both of you had been entered into a contest not of your own choosing too. Though it's been an exhausting experience, first Kaine, and then you, I feel like I've graduated with a PhD. in *Loving and Techniques.*

"I've been exposed to extensive and explosive carnal knowledge, by two world travelers, so much so that I have quickly become a sexually sophisticated woman doing sexual acts in places and in ways I've never imagined," she explained walking around the chair.

He reached out and pulled on her wrist inviting her to make a nest on his lap. She wrapped her arms around his shoulders.

Luka looked into her eyes and explained.

"I don't want you to get the wrong idea. I don't expect, nor want you any other way than how you are. I don't want you to worry about how I feel about loving you. I appreciate that you're open to suggestions and adventures. It makes everything I share with you more fun and pleasurable for me, and I hope the same for you too because I'm sharing me with you, and my ways to enjoy loving.

"I hear how much you enjoy what you and I share. It makes the pleasure stronger because I also feel how our loving delights you. Your words tell me, your face and body show me."

"But really Angel Eyes, you've had to teach me to use my words, to show you my feelings and how my body reacts to your touch."

"I'm sorry, Babe, that I misread your willingness and tenderness as experience."

She knew he loved her words because he was growing under her derrière.

"Being willing and becoming adventurous to explore sexual pleasure has come from the amazing experience of feeling safe with Kaine. He taught me how to trust him and indulge in the pure, unquenchable pleasures of my body with his, anywhere, anyway. The tenderness was from Jon."

She felt him growing more. She stroked his hair, and her fingertip detailed his facial features. She wondered if he'd purposely sent her to Kaine for sex lessons. Not a ridiculous conclusion in light of his recent admissions. He'd understood that morning in Chelsea that she was inexperienced when it came to sex. Must have believed that Kaine would find that attractive and sent her to please him. However, there was really no way to know how Luka thought about anything.

She ran her fingers over his face that sported a light day's growth of beard making him feel rough. "I wish I could say making love with you was from more experience. But I loved Jon for a long time. It wasn't difficult to remember how to care for someone.

"I've always had the philosophy if I found a man — I mean the right man — I wanted to enjoy sex with, I wouldn't be frigid. If he was worth undressing for, I had better enjoy it and make damn sure it was the same for him."

"That Babe is a wonderfully healthy attitude. But this changes an essential and important part of our relationship."

Holly jerked, wondering what.

Luka quickly responded. "No Babe, a good part. First, I don't think we need to use protection any longer. I've been regularly tested for HIV and sexually transmitted diseases, and I'm clean. I know Kaine was tested; we went together before the tour for insurance purposes. And he's such a fanatic and paranoid. I don't think he's had time for sex while he was putting together the tour. And if he did, it was definitely safe sex, well, except for the obvious time. That's another story.

"Since he's the only man you've been with and Jon was long ago. You're already pregnant, what is the use for them? If you trust me that I'm telling the truth, it will be bloody fantastic to feel me inside you." His eyes sparkled, and they were a beautiful atmospheric blue.

She needed to be realistic to pull off the charade. For the next forty-eight hours, if Luka were anything like Kaine, he'd expect lots of sex with her, depending on his stamina, and his suggestion sounded logical to stop working with the cumbersome sheaths.

"It is all right with me if we dispense with them. Kaine was exceptionally concerned with protection, and I've often wondered how I got pregnant." She watched Luka's sparkle wane with words of Kaine.

His eyes were filled with a shadow of a doubt. Luka looked into her eyes and spoke with a stammer. "As do I ... maybe, it was planned?"

Again, Holly saw it there. What everyone spoke of, the intense competition. But planned? After everything, she'd heard it would not surprise her. Kaine had been insistent about having babies and wanted her pregnant, but to be cowardly and brutal to take her without consent?

But she knew he'd never expected her to say no in the first place, no one ever had. Maybe he wouldn't have gone about it his way if she'd agreed. Again, she wondered if it was the game, the checkmate to Luka, believing that Luka would never take her any way he could — baby and all.

And how could she answer? Kaine had been a fantastic lover, draped in a fairy tale setting. But Kaine hadn't been real either. For the moment, sitting on Luka's lap was her reality.

Luka had been correct that she would never forget Christmas Eve. Luka was certainly the more determined lover, but Kaine was more passionate, a sweeter lover motivated by his open heart. It was difficult to answer which was the better lover. But because with Kaine it had been a sweeter love, with both of their hearts open heart-to-heart, she would always prefer Kaine.

And then Holly realized that's what made her the heart of the *Hurri-Kaine*, not due to Luka's creative headline.

There was a missing piece of the puzzle, explaining why Luka had made love Christmas Eve with such control over her. She knew, this time, the ghost of Kaine had been trailing Luka too. He'd been trying to best Kaine.

Luka wanted to prove to her that he was the better lover. She wondered if his brilliant lovemaking would change when there was nothing to prove.

Holly wrapped her arms protectively around his head, cradling him, pressing him harder to her bosom, kissing the top of his head.

Holly lifted Luka's chin with a bent finger and drank slowly from his soft, sweet peppermint flavored lips.

Showtime!

Chapter Nine

BEST OF MY LOVE

Holly wasn't tired anymore.

Luka wasn't tired anymore either, judging by the bulge under her derrière. Luka was hers, ripe for the taking. His kiss told her that along with his eyes that said he'd never leave her. Her body swelled with desire for him. She looked into his blue eyes she would have once died for and confirmed in a whisper, "Though this has all been orchestrated, what choice I've had was right."

Luka smiled and then said to create a bit of mystery.

"I haven't given you my last Christmas present." Luka raised his chin. His eyes glowed intensely with want.

And for a moment, the hot blast of light frightened her, yet hypnotized her at the same time. How could this man want her that much? How ruggedly sexy he looked wearing a sand colored Levi shirt inviting her like his succulent plump lips. The rough leather of his vest a quick reminder of his swiftly growing passion, a result of the seriousness with which he looked at her as if she was prey about to be devoured. Why was she always mesmerized by his strong magic? The way he would go after her, even crawl on his hands and knees to get to her. And she remembered the first time they were together in London at her hotel room. That glorious morning when Luka crawled across her bed to her because he'd wanted her.

Holly struggled for breath from the reminder of what lay in store for her. But this Luka was different. This man recently shared some of his darkest secrets. This Luka would be ready to convince her to keep them. He'd trusted her.

To make love with a man that trusted her, especially a powerful man like Luka, demanded that her new role as a dutiful concubine should start unbuttoning the first of many on her blouse.

Luka spoke softly but with command.

"No, let me. I want to unwrap my Christmas present myself. Slowly. I want to enjoy each precious moment."

His hand followed after hers before she could react to his potent words, for he knew her well enough that she would recoil from his heady words and drew her near, closer.

She felt his shield of heat, closer still until she inhaled his fresh sweet scent, closer still until her lips were a breath away from his.

It wasn't clear which one would move first.

Luka was locked in an enchantment that froze the moment as he gazed deep into her eyes. There he found the reflection of the deceitful secrets he'd shared. His eyes saying he was wondering if it was time to celebrate the safety of being accepted for who he was. He moved closer and placed his lips on hers. Easily at first, then as if to challenge her, afraid that if he let go his ugly secrets would force her to leave, and he would lose her forever.

Holly latched onto Luka's lips, covering his, demanding to feel his tongue.

Luka was seemingly relieved she would respond to his kiss and gave her what she wanted.

Her hand moved up to cup his face.

His hand steadied her, twisted her, bringing her back down on his lap. He cradled her, kissing her as he unbuttoned her blouse, then pulled it and her bra off her, dropping them on the floor.

And she was lost. Each time Luka touched her, she found a new undiscovered depth. She kissed him with more enthusiasm, surprised by how many layers of passion lay waiting. His experienced hand had her exposed to his fleshy touch as she sank into the abyss of his kiss. She survived on one breath, for she dared not break the moment. She felt safe riding the bliss of a trusting Luka. How unusual the moment was, to touch Luka, to feel his pureness wash all over her. No fear, no restraint, pure Luka ... devil or angel.

Luka loved her, his hand caressed her skin, running lightly over the crest of her nipples, back and forth, slowly, until she felt the burn melting her core and she squeezed her legs together. But it didn't ease the sting.

She felt Luka smiling in the kiss. He knew what he was doing.

His hand cupped her breast from the bottom and squeezed the hardened peak, as it popped up in the circle of his forefinger and thumb, a tiny volcano ready to explode.

And explode she did as Luka swiftly broke the kiss and latched onto her nipple. She moaned and instantly arched her back into him as an instant reflex.

His mouth open and took more.

She arched again.

Luka knew exactly what he was doing and what it was doing to her.

It was simply impossible to resist him. And after the fiery moment, he released her nipple like a cork from a bottle. His long gleaming hair slipped from behind his ears. He leveled his chin and his gaze locked onto hers with those hot blue eyes, beautiful eyes to-die-for.

She held no breath, nothing to sustain her as he studied her eyes. She was dizzy, spinning, as if about to lose consciousness. But he wouldn't let her.

Luka shook her, reviving her. His hand slid down her slim hip, and he fanned his fingers to cover the top of her thigh.

As if stung, she lurched under his touch.

His hand moved quickly, underneath her skirt and moved with even greater speed than her pleasure, leaving a trail of tiny fires. His fingers lifted the band of her lace panties and slipped inside as quickly.

She got her wish and reached up to show him how good he felt, how exquisitely he moved inside her.

"No, forget about me," he pleaded, "Enjoy my touch, my gift to you. I want to enjoy my Christmas present."

Holly closed her eyes for she hadn't the strength to show him the depths he'd already reached in her. She tried to breathe and fill her lungs to show him with her body how he made her feel. How each stroke of his fingers coaxed waves of shivers and show him how beautiful he made her feel.

This was beautiful Luka. Of course, there was always the question of how much to show Luka?

How much did she really want to reveal?

How much did he deserve to know?

And how much of what existed between them was true?

There was one way to find out — when Luka filled her inside, showing her, the best way he knew, how much he loved her.

Her smile grew larger anticipating what was waiting for her. She recognized this feeling; it was this way with Kaine. And the thought sent shock waves through her, alerting her mind, events were becoming too familiar.

She spotted Kaine when she opened her eyes. Yes, Kaine lurked in the shadows, leaning on the wall. One of his long, trouser draped legs bent and the shoe heel rested against the wall. He wore a dark red pullover sweater with his arms crossed over his magnificent chest and his eyes watching, filled with bewilderment. His dark hair, long, loose about his shoulders and blown back as if a breeze dared to kiss his handsome, romantic face.

He was doing it again, invading her thoughts, reminding, his return was imminent.

He wanted to know why she wasn't home waiting for him? She felt the hair rise on the back of her neck.

She'd no way to explain to the ghost of Kaine that to get to him, to protect them all, she needed to keep Luka satisfy.

He couldn't interfere with these moments.

She had to focus on Luka.

She shook her head as if to tell Kaine to go farther into the shadows.

But he was tenacious.

All right.

Holly warned the invader in her mind.

Watch.

See if that makes you happy.

Holly turned all her attention to Luka. His fingers, encouraged by her response, removed the panties and skirt until she lay across Luka, giving herself up as the blood sacrifice. Her clothes lay in a pile on the floor at his feet. She dressed in Kaine's gift, the diamond stud earring.

Luka flicked her long hair to the side to look his fill. His annoyed expression vanished as he scrutinized the length of her body and his fingertips followed the trail of his eyes.

He stopped his fingers, paused, building the anticipation and then plunged them inside her. This was what he'd called her being willing, able to respond his way. She arched, and the sacrificial moan escaped.

She watched him.

He plunged again. He'd approved.

She arched, her eyes locked onto his.

She arched again.

He watched. His erection stabbed her back as she relaxed between each stroke.

The rub by his fingertip was becoming a white-hot agony. Her back rubbed the length of his rigid sex. The motion became maddening as his breath quicken, blowing about her warm, and fast.

His chest moved in and out.

Every muscle in her body aware of the motion of thrusting and withdrawal.

The lunge.

The thrusts.

The peak.

And then sweet peace.

She needed her lips crowning his stiff sex. She rubbed her back alongside him, marveling at the size he could grow. How had he ever fit? But she was twisting up inside, and the heat burned steady, threatening to blast her. She needed to move things along quickly. Luka was moving far too slowly, savoring far too many moments. The plane would be landing soon and then he would stop his devilishly, sinful, hot touch.

She attempted to sit.

His forearm kept her in place. "Do this for me luv. Let me take my time. This is an unexpected delight. Let me show how I feel and then if you want, you can touch me."

"You want to make me scream?"

"I hope so luv, I hope so."

After all his ugly confessions, how had it become possible to become this open and close to unadulterated malevolence? She continued to wonder between the rushes of heat.

Luka kept kissing her, dropping her down another notch, showing her new depths to her feelings. And then due to all he'd confessed to her, she'd a feeling Luka was going to fuck her beyond the place called Oblivion.

"Can I enjoy my present any way I want?" He advanced with persistence.

"We're going to land soon," she prompted half in protest, half in submission.

"Who owns the plane?" He quietly reminded.

She opened her lust-flooded eyes and stared into a blurry version of Luka. She'd heard his words. And she was pleased he owned CMT because he could do whatever the hell he wanted. The faint smile on her face must have told him, he was right of course.

Luka lifted her, maneuvering her right leg over his lap, spreading her thighs apart, mere inches from his fully clad sex. She looked down and watched his hand unbutton his Levi's with the ease she would know one day. Practice did make perfect. She saw the tip of his pink sex spring into view.

Hurry!

He was close. Which of his many tricks would he delight her with next?

She closed her eyes.

"No, don't look away," Luka insisted.

"You're my present. I want to pleasure you. Watch you."

His hand slipped up her chest to hold her about the throat. His strong hand fanned around her neck, and he held on tight.

A curious place to brace himself. But Luka knew tricks, and this would be new. She felt the heat flush her body as the tip of his sex touched her aching bud. She shuddered when Luka squeezed her neck. She felt like she was dangling from the bough of a hanging tree.

Luka touched her again with the thick-skinned tip, and she groaned. Each time her body shuddered, she squirmed trying to slide on to him. But Luka held her, his grip about her throat tighter, his other hand guiding his mushroomed tip to touch her, to brush against her, teasing, rubbing, and ripening her for the kill. He was strong, physically strong to hold her in place.

The pressure became unbearable. Her hands were rolled into balls pressing on his shoulders. His strong, unbelievably strong hand were holding her up, his other was rubbing her sex faster and faster.

"Luka please." She heard herself beg.

"I can't hear you, Babe."

"Luka, I ache. I'm burning inside — either stop or fuck me!"

"Which do you want from me, my luv?"

"I want this."

Her hand fell into his lap, and she tightly wrapped it around his powerful shaft forcing him to loosen his grip on her neck, straightened his legs out forward and she slid down the front of him like water cascading over a familiar ledge.

She slid onto her knees as he opened his legs. Before Mr. Hunter could object, his Christmas present had his stiff determination locked inside her mouth. She sucked him in and moaned. Again, and again, she sucked him until she could hear the sounds of pleasure lost in the caverns of his chest.

Well, that was a start!

Holly wanted his deep groans of pleasure loud, loud enough to fill the jet's cabin. She would draw the truth of his desire from him. This was where she was most comfortable. Her hand stroked the plump pink sac beneath and then his shaft with a split mind.

She focused on one thought, to drive Luka out of his mind with pleasure. And what better way? Wasn't the way to a man's heart through his virility?

Or, was it stomach?

According to the always-attractive Mr. Hunter, not all the sex around the world had claimed his heart. But then again, after his latest confessions, the jury was out on whether he had a heart.

He moaned again. Yes, there was no doubt how much Luka like her mouth and lips.

Her tongue lashed him properly, and the sighs of pleasure were creeping up his chest. Each a tiny bit louder than the last. And that was fine, he'd taught her well, she liked this slow.

She never seemed to tire of the sucking motion, or the taste of him, the strength of his mighty muscle and the heat of it. Yes, this was where she felt most comfortable, with this nearness to his body scented with musk.

Holly opened her eyes to look at a wall of tight flesh, the light trail of hair. Her eyes followed the trail where it joined a thin valley of short dark blonde hair. Was everything about Luka sexy, beautiful, an erotic turn on?

Feeling him in her mouth, her free hand followed her lips squeezing a bit tighter. His moans of pleasure grew louder but remained lodged in his upper body.

Holly moved to get comfortable pulling him with her. It would seem this loving task would require steadiness and needed to pace herself.

"Enough...." she heard him say between pants.

But Holly continued.

"No. You're my Christmas present, and I want you to stop. I don't want to hurry."

She'd barely let go before he was pulling her to him.

He was strong.

She smiled, reading his mind.

He wanted her over his lap.

She tried to throw a leg over him.

But he surprised her. He turned her around, placing her back against the trunk of his body. The shirt and vest felt rough against her back. But not for long. He bent her forward as if he wanted her forehead to touch her knees.

Ummm

Holly felt the sturdy tip of his rock hard sex, moving the length of her swollen lips. One hand held her at the back of her neck, and his other hand guided his strong shaft inside her one burning inch at a time. He allowed his moans to escape, sounding as if he were being burnt by her wetness as he entered her.

And the maddening slowness burned her too.

He moved in another inch and stopped.

She heard the escaping sounds of enjoyment loud and clear in the cabin — they were hers.

Luka moved a bit more.

"Luka ... do ... it. Please?" She jerked her head back planning to sit up and slide down the length of his formidable power. But she knew, he knew, how maddening the waiting was. He knew exactly what he was doing. Without warning, she was moving forward, and any second would crash on the floor.

What the hell was he doing?

"Luka, I'm falling."

And then she wasn't falling anymore. She hit the floor on her belly with a thud, bringing Luka, falling on top, behind her, as his stiff shaft jammed in her, repeatedly until she heard one moan after another, and they were all hers. His hand wrapped around under the front of her, cupping her breasts, his forehead braced against her neck. This man was bent on fucking her beyond Oblivion.

She saw the signpost ahead.

She felt like an animal, raw and hungry.

He plunged her into depths she would have never believed existed. No wonder Luka had been private about his feelings. To be this vulnerable, meant he'd once loved openly, profoundly. And she felt the trust from him, oozing from his sentiment as his body enchanted her, enjoying his Christmas present, lunging again and again, with the quickness she wanted to put out the fire. He was moving with rough jerks. One hand moved up her chest to her neck once again. He arched her back and then he moved further into her. She heard her sighs telling him she loved doing this with him. His hand slipped to her chin then she twisted her upper torso. She could feel his full, wet lips blowing hot puffs of breaths on her cheek as his masculine scent swept over her face.

He moved easily, in and out of her body. His lips slid to her ear and slightly missing their mark, he crawled up on his knees, bringing her with him placing her on her knees, all the while shoving in inch-by-inch, shoving himself higher and higher into her, setting a maddening pace.

She was slowly crawling forward on her hands and knees until her head hit the cabin wall.

He pinned her with his solid love, impaling her.

Holly didn't quite know from which end the flame ignited. But when it crashed in the middle of her sensitive wet core, squeezed him, the fire exploded causing a meltdown around his mighty, stiff sex. As the moist lubricant of her release started to surround Luka, she felt the wondrous and magnificent power of being a woman.

Satisfied sounds slipped out, groans from his inner core

as Luka exploded inside her.

The chamber filled quickly. Luka froze in her body.

She followed him.

Her body melting like wax from the wick. She melted into his skin to become one.

And her mind was blown to Oblivion where she found Luka standing, smiling, waiting for her, leaning on the signpost.

Luka was certainly like no previous lover. Was Kaine's ghost watching? The son-of-a-bitch had given her to Luka, what did he expect? Did he think he could do better than Luka? She doubted it.

Luka moved, thrusting again, locked in that state of oblivion, rocking, plunging, filling, and exploding again.

Holly laid counting Luka's warm breaths, blowing heavily in her ear, lying on the floor of the CMT jet, marveling at the expression of his intense sexual desire for her, high above the clouds with the Christmas Star as a witness.

Chapter Ten

BABY I'M GONNA LEAVE YOU

W hy did he behave this way?
"No!"
"Why?" she demanded.

"I can't do it again, Holly."

Uh oh, he'd used her name. That meant serious business. What the hell, she'd try again. "Please, one more time?"

"The plane is going to land, this time, Babe. I had the pilot circle for as long as allowed."

He'd used his, 'please listen to reason' voice.

"Tell him to circle until I'm done with you. We need enough time to fuck again!" There, she'd challenged him with such authority. It seemed indecent how quickly she wanted him again. She decided on one last plea.

"You own the damn plane! I thought you promised to make me happy?"

"No more!" He declared with a chuckle as if he'd forgotten he owned the plane.

"How long then?" She demanded.

"Less than an hour, don't worry. I have an hour left of

Christmas with my favorite present." He insisted with a sexy smile.

"Maybe Santa will give you a little extra time."

"I expected Santa to give me what I wanted for Christmas." Luka maintained, his eyes flashing wild as if thinking about a new adventure for her.

Holly waited impatiently at the private landing strip. Luka picked up a brand-new, black, four-wheeled drive Jeep waiting at the Tucson airport. He followed the map Michael gave him until they'd found the address. What a mansion, expensive and skillful in design. The desert landscape looked like a slice out of the old west. The cactus raised their hands up into the night sky like prisoners in a holdup. The inviting surrounding countryside complimented the giant multi-level executive home like an apron. The custom built home resembled an Adobe Indian dwelling.

The interior displayed large, spacious, vaulted ceilings with scattered skylights. The shiny Spanish-tiled floors echoed with Luka's boot heels all about the house. Dark lacquered, wood molding trimmed the stucco walls throughout the numerous rooms. The southwest styled, leather furniture was white eggshell set within a color palette of corals, desert greens, and turquoise designs woven as accent colors throughout the house. Holly delighted in the ultra-modern electric kitchen, stocked and ready for any occasion. They chose the spacious upstairs master bedroom suite to call their love nest. A beautiful geometric layout and design, it came complete with a fireplace and whirlpool in the giant spa and bath area. It also entertained an incredible, breathtaking view of the Tucson Valley, from the windows that ran three stories high and the length of one entire wall.

After catching her breath, Holly ran a whirlpool bath, scenting it with the supplied Desert Rose bath salts. She sat by the tub. For a split second, she remembered London and the strong scent of lavender. But she needed to dismiss the lone memory while stripping and then stepping into the bubbles. Holly looked up to find him. She made the decision to make the best of this situation.

Holly needed to accept Luka's advances for less than forty-eight hours. Not a terrible task, to feast on Luka's gorgeous, nude body, standing in the doorway wearing nothing but a gold medallion, gold hoop earring, and turquoise necklace.

Her tired, sore, and worn out body wanted more of him. Her eyes must have told him the same because he started to swell and there wasn't anything more beautiful than Luka half-aroused. That reminded her of wrapping her lips around his growing shaft and making him strong. But he always took his time to make love, and normally she would have delighted in the adventure, but right then, her pregnant body seemed on overloaded with exhaustion.

Luka sauntered over, stepped in, parting the bubbles, coming close, so close. His usually bright shining eyes were cool, piercing.

"Make love to me Luka, but promise me one thing?"

"What does my Christmas present want from me? Ask it's yours."

Holly smiled at his chivalry. "Don't take long? I'm tired and sore from your loving, but I want to love you. I need to fall asleep with you inside me."

"Is this the pregnancy talking?"

"I'm not sure. This is new for me as well, but I can't get

enough of you. I long for you. My body is as if it's in a perpetual state of heat. A hot fever is trapped under my skin."

His fingers responded to her words, by tracing the tips of her overly sensitive nipples.

"And this — is it better or worse because you're pregnant?"

"I can describe it as every fiber of my being is on fire — maybe more intense due to of the heightened sensitivity from the pregnancy. But most likely the cause is you and the ways you love me."

There, he'd wanted her words, and she'd said them always surprised how easy it was to allow him to believe that he could draw her most personal thoughts from her.

Luka smiled and pushed his body into hers. His strong love pressed, threatening to devour her.

"I wonder what my excuse is. I don't have the pregnancy to blame. It must be your hot, wet, and tight little body, Babe." While he spoke, his hand moved to cover her. And when he'd said hot, his fingers plunged inside her and left them there and confessed.

"I can't wait to be inside you again. It's been too long since I've been able to forget condoms. I'm like a starving man at a feast with you, Babe."

"You do have a flair with words Mr. Hunter." She pointed out while the fire from his fingers ignited her more.

He smiled graciously at her compliment. "I've remembered a few more things I'd like to show you."

Holly should have purred because she counted on Luka to astound her.

He moved, pulling his fingers from her. He chose a

large loofah and passed it across a turquoise-colored bar of sweetly scented soap. He started to wash her flesh delicately moving all around her body like a skilled masseuse, washing every crevasse and valley of her body. How well he recognized her vulnerabilities under his seductive touch.

After they'd exhausted the bath, he stepped out, and curiously gazed at her.

"I want to teach you about how I like to look at you."

The shivers ran rampant along her skin at that thought. She learned quickly that Luka indulged in a sensual extravagance that engaged all of his senses. He'd taught her his love of hearing the words of sex, the sounds, and cries. He added the visual. His seemed fascinated with the changes in her breasts and nipples, but mostly he loved to suck on her inflamed bud. There he activated all of his senses. He loved to touch her, everywhere, inside her and with long, languid strokes. The plunging motion seemed to give him great pleasure. She looked at him and sighed.

He stood near the vanity.

She rose up out of the water. She stepped out to pause on the rug placed around the tub.

"Babe, stand there. Let me take my fill. Let me look at you."

She stood flushed with embarrassment at first. But he'd made a reasonable request. She'd wanted the same of him. Luka's sensual gaze washed over her, putting her at ease, as her body naturally molded into a centerfold pose. But, wondered what to do when the heat inside her became too untenable.

"Sit on the edge of the tub. Open your legs, I want to see all of you." He instructed.

Would the heat ever stop flushing her cheeks? She opened her legs a bit, but his hand motioned directing her to open wider. Again, she did, and again wider.

He stood looking at her and then directed her. "Arch your back." After a while, the glow in his eyes lessened, then shook his head as he testified.

"You're fucking beautiful."

He sighed, moved closer, and picked up the nearby towel to pat her dry. When he finished, he dusted the curves of her body with a wonderfully aromatic powder, from the Desert Rose bath set. And then he rested his hand on her lower abdomen.

"You're a first, my luv. With all my travels, I've never been with a pregnant woman. What you must be experiencing, life growing inside you, and that makes me jealous, and it angers me that Kaine stole this precious time from me."

Holly stood quietly, realizing what created his obsessive fascination with her body. That she carried life. The rare glimpse into him at that moment was important, but his words couldn't have shocked her more.

"I want to fuck you hard until I replace his baby with mine. I want you to bear my children, my beauty. Lots of them." He looked at her, but his hand continued to rub the swelling of her belly in large sensuous circles.

"Do I frighten you with my honesty?"

"I have to say yes. We try not to speak his name. It's like tempting his ghost here."

"I'm not convinced we'll ever be free of Kaine. He's been in my life for as long as I care to remember. My mate, the closest man to me for a long while. And knowing he has stolen this precious time from me, it's fitting that I watch his child growing inside you, and then assume the role of father. His child will be enough of a constant reminder."

That last confession didn't sound like a good thing.

Her internal warning system announced, on high alert, loud and clear. Something sounded wrong.

... enough of a constant reminder.

His hands roamed her ribs and then up to her swollen breasts, full from the pregnancy and affirmed, "Your breasts seem fuller even more than a day ago. The nipples have grown larger as well. You're becoming more beautiful by the day, making me want a family. Something once dreamed of, then forgotten."

Luka's voice trailed, and the blistering memory crossed his eyes leaving a trail of stubborn tears.

Holly stepped up close to Luka, taking him in her arms to comfort him.

He dropped his forehead to her shoulder. His hands slid around her and then he placed his arm under her knees and lifted her. He took a few strides to the king-size four-post bed.

Luka reprogrammed the *Bon Jour* CD, punching in their favorite love making song. The song they made love to for hours in the canyon that morning. Luka looked down to her as he stood at the edge of the bed and laid her down gently.

"Time isn't up, you're still my Christmas present?"

"Every day."

He smiled.

His subsequent words blew her away.

"I'm glad you're here with me. I never thought this

would happen. You're everything I've ever wanted, and I have looked for you for such a long time, and I'd lost hope, no longer believing you existed." He stepped back. His divine body shimmered, luminous from the light of the dancing flames from the adobe fireplace. Then he pulled back the drapes and the astounding backdrop behind Luka paled in comparison. On the horizon, the twinkling lights of Tucson nestled in the foothills at his feet. He leaned one knee on the bed.

Holly moved with the swoosh of his body weight forcing the bed to give, welcoming his arrival. The usual hot, sweeping desire flew with speed through her body until the heat rose to an inferno.

"Well, maybe not too quickly." She invited, knowing it would be another long night of Luka moving freely inside her.

Chapter Eleven

YOU'RE THE BEST THING

Five Days — Kaine

A brilliant desert sunray awoke Holly from her peaceful slumber. The streams of golden light bursting in from the coral-tinted sky dusted the outline of the majestic mountain range. The black outline of the cactus stood tall, straight like centurions greeting the morning sun.

Holly quickly glanced over to Luka, peacefully sleeping. He'd nothing to prove to her last night. His loving tender and sweet resulted in her feeling closer to him than at any other time. She leaned in a bit, to lay her head on his fragrant chest.

"Ummm," she whispered, remembering the tenderness of the sweet love they made, long before the clock struck midnight leaving them exhausted. She glanced at the clock, they'd slept for ten hours.

Luka acknowledged her sigh because he moved. And

being rested, rejuvenated, and adventurous, he started to trace the hot lines of her body as if to invite her to make love one more time. But with a full shooting scheduled that day, the clock declared there was no more time.

Holly rose and noticed hanging in the closet a thick, red, and gray striped robe, beautifully handcrafted she assumed from a blanket by a native tribe, wrapped it around her, and then slipped her feet into delicately crafted beaded moccasins.

She hurried downstairs to the all-electric kitchen. There she rustled up strawberries and granola. She set a kettle of water to heat for tea. She took the freshly brewed Red-Raspberry tea that scented the kitchen, and a plate of sliced apples and pineapple out quickly to the enclosed dining area that overlooked the bountiful chaparral of the Tucson basin. Such quiet beauty. Life there seemed wonderfully refreshing, and a dramatic change from dirty, traffic-ridden L.A. The most that happened was the sagebrush blowing by captured by the soft desert wind.

She sighed and then hearing movement behind her, turned in time to watch Luka's elegant entrance. When he came into view, his golden hair hung tussled, and he wore a pair of 501, Levi's that he'd didn't finish buttoning. The top golden hair peeked out the V of his pant. She shook her head. The enticing sight of him sent an immediate wake-up call to her. There should be a law about a man that he can't be as stunning as Luka first thing in the morning.

"Good morning, Papa Bear." She playfully responded for no particular reason, except to express her total comfort with him.

"I like the sound of that." He sighed approvingly with a

breathy morning voice.

"What?"

"You called me Papa Bear. Sounds native, or like ... someone with bloody roots, like, someone who belongs somewhere." He leaned and kissed her a long, heartwarming good morning kiss.

She looked up at him, inches from his face. "To wake up with you every morning is going to be problematic. Do you always look good enough to eat?"

He leaned in and kissed her quickly again, to reward her choice of words. "You're bloody good for me!"

Luka pulled his briefcase to the counter and took out his phone. She'd lost him for a while and thought to do the same and check her faxes. She'd sent her assistant Lucy to England on a top-secret mission to ferret out the mystery to the Ghost of Briarwood, and anything available on the enigmatic, Mr. Hunter. And she hoped Lucy contacted her with news.

Holly headed off to prepare for the day. After a quick shower, she pulled on a pair of rust-colored corduroy pants and an over-sized, camel-colored cable knitted sweater. She slipped on two-inch black, suede ankle boots. She'd decided to wear her hair free and wavy. Then thought no, instead, would blend in with the local atmosphere better by weaving her dark, mid-back length hair, into long plaits and then wrapped the ends with leather, beaded ties.

Holly stood ready for the fax machine. Luka ordered the background check on *Bon Jour* assembled and faxed. A poor intern in L.A. needed to be called Christmas day with instructions to go in at the crack of dawn this morning and dig up this information for her.

She secretly hoped Lucy came up with something because the mystery made her determined to get to the bottom of it. That damn ghost of Briarwood somehow exiled her from Kaine.

She assembled her questions and then music sheets and sat down to rehearse on guitar for a while. Jaden Moore, the singer for *Bon Jour*, would be out early afternoon and then leave for a sound check. She had forty-five minutes to rehearse and get the show in the can.

The faxes from CMT arrived on time and delighted. Holly read the news from Lucy.

> **Hunter not last name. SINCLARE birth name.**
> **Daughter of local midwife ready to reveal important**
> **information for a price.**
> **Await instructions.**

"SINCLARE?" she stated aloud. No wonder she hadn't found anything on him. He'd listed the holdings under his father's surname — *his* surname. Well, she would have to investigate this.

She faxed Lucy.

> **Follow paper trail of Sinclare.**
> **Pay anything for information.**

Holly sat down to play every number one hit of *Bon Jour's* included in the package Michael gave to Luka. She didn't need a preview of the new CD, she'd personally experienced them with Luka, on Christmas Eve. When she'd finished, she noted the silence. She looked around the room. What was Luka doing?

Luka Sinclare?

More mystery.

More questions.

But, they needed to wait.

Holly noticed the video crew outback setting up by the pool area. She listened to the familiar voice of her lover doing what he did best, shouting orders, deciding on the light and best camera angles. She walked over to the sliding glass doors.

Luka called out to her and for the first time, he called her by his pet name not caring who noticed. "Hey Babe, come here ... tell me what you think?"

Holly glanced about at the mostly male crew. They certainly didn't miss the endearment, she and Luka, not a secret anymore.

As Luka encouraged her, they worked as a team, creating a mini set for her.

"This show is pivotal, important," he explained.

"If it goes as I have planned, we will take the show out on location more often, giving it a broader range and budget."

"You're always thinking and never satisfied." She insisted sending a knowing wink directed to him.

"Oh yeah? Why do I bloody well sense there's a challenge in that?" He queried as he grabbed her behind with a tight grip.

Her face blushes in front of the crew. What happened to the reserved Englishman she'd come to expect in public? This man claimed what's his and didn't care about repercussions. However, grabbing her butt in public would certainly never be a favored reaction from him. It reminded her of being property again, and she would have to point that out later. But then she thought to forgive him. He looked darn cute wearing his Ray Ban sunglasses, black cowboy hat, and a white crisp cowboy shirt with a black leather vest lined with sheep's wool. He'd worn her favorite bun-hugging black Levi's, with black boots. His hair hung free, blowing in the cold and crisp desert wind.

She did decide to caution him as if he'd gone and done it.

"You shouldn't have grabbed me."

His clear blue eyes challenged hers.

Holly pulled Luka's hips to hers and kissed his neck. She looked at him again. They challenged her. She kissed his chin. She looked again into his eyes that said he'd go as far as she dared. She pressed her lips to his and watched his eyes close. She followed and opened her mouth, and he followed her lead, as she dipped in to kiss him deeply. He joined her and filled her mouth, as she boldly wrapped her leg around his, holding on to his waist with her hands, knowing … she would leave him.

She quickly forgot the crew, the birds that flew overhead, and the sun as it shone brightly on their heated kiss. She followed him into oblivion, deeper into Luka, where his pure love flowed freely.

Luka gave in first. He stepped back coming up for air.

She grinned with satisfaction.

"Ah, everything secure on the set? Holly needs me." He claimed boldly.

No one challenged him. Carl, the lead man, shouted back.

"We're fine Luka. We have about an hour until Jaden arrives. We'll order in lunch."

"Why don't you chaps go out?" Luka suggested as he dug in his pocket extracting a hundred-dollar bill.

"Go check out the locals."

The crewmembers took the hint and Luka wrapped his arm around Holly's waist as he walked her toward the house. They passed the sunken living room, playfully fighting to touch each other. She slapped Luka's hand that threatened to pinch her butt. Holly laughed joyously all the way to the master suite where they no longer waited to undress each other.

It took too much time.

Chapter Twelve

SWEET LOVE

Holly eagerly met Luka in the middle of the king-sized bed. Their arms surrounded each other, pulling until their bodies touched.

His eyes searched hers. "I hope you believe me, I need you, Babe."

"Yes, you do, Angel Eyes."

Holly watched Luka close them and opened his mouth to cover hers. And as promised, the hot shivers shot through her body. His hand went up to her sensitive breasts, and she bit his lips from the flood of sensations. Her leg squeezed in between his, placing him closer to her lower body if possible. She wanted to be as close as she could get to him. Her hand traveled from his hair to the top of his shoulders where it slipped down between the two of them to the hardness of him. There she traced the inside of his leg giving her a moment to catch her breath.

Holly's heart skipped a beat, her stomach maintained butterflies as she touched him. Too long since she tasted him, and she broke the kiss and went to his neck. She spent a little time, quickly kissing him to the trail of dark blond hair that always led her to his pink and ready sex. Her body ran wet and ready for him, and she sank, drowning in a heat of excitement.

She paused to look at him, thankful for the light of day. As usual, he appeared incredibly beautiful. She'd become a quick study when it came to looking at Luka. She found his eyes watching her. He'd taught her that he liked to look at her. She would allow him to watch. She held his stare as she placed her tongue on the commanding tip and licked. She would watch his face for as long as possible.

Luka didn't move, his beautiful bedroom eyes flared with lust, and his ash-colored eyelashes lazily opened and closed. Occasionally, he sighed in response to her talent, but his hands no longer sought to twist in her hair.

Holly kissed and held him with her hand as she lifted his sex into his full view.

She watched his facial expressions as she placed her mouth over him and drew in gradually and then firmly.

She watched the dark liquid pools of his eyes vanish slowly, then open, fix on her, firing her desire up three notches.

She watched his chest rising and falling, faster and faster until he no longer drew a breath of air without parting his lips as she sucked longer until she captured him in her mouth.

And she watched as he parted his lips wider, trying to draw short puffs of air and then he surrendered to a pant.

Her whole body burned on fire for him.

She watched his eyes and enticing him empowered her, inviting him to fly off the edge from the pleasure she lavished on him.

He closed his eyes again, and his back arched, his neck stretched to show her his throbbing veins.

She sucked harder and harder, and her body trembled inside at the sight of him almost ready to release. He glowed with the light of day as the perspiration obediently rose to bead all over his body.

Holly's hand glided up his slick wet skin over his ribcage then higher to where she started to keep rhythm with his heartbeat. She sucked as forceful as possible. His whole body stiffened. She could tell by his face it would happen soon, and yes, she understood he would let it happen naturally.

Holly kept his rhythm, timing herself to him. Slowly he opened his eyes to look into hers as she continued staying with him. She closed her eyes and opened them again.

He reached out for her. But she shied away from his touch signaling that she would not stop. His seed spilled a little at a time as he tried to control it.

She let loose on him and fiercely sucked with demand until he no longer had any choice left. She needed to make adjustment unable to take all of his enormous size into her mouth, yet she stayed with him.

And when he grabbed her and squeezed until she thought he would crush her bones, she stayed. She stayed when his body stiffened, and he latched onto the end of one braid.

She stayed as she listened to the sounds bubble up from his throat to rattle the walls. She stayed with him until he opened his eyes and looked down into hers, with those beautiful sexy blue eyes.

"Come to me, Babe." He summoned between breaths.

His breathy voice calling to her, absent of harshness, no command, but an invitation laced with a tone of appreciation.

She looked up at him, and his arms stretched out waiting for her.

"Please, let me love you," he begged as he wound the long plaited braid around his hand, reeling her closer to him.

That's all it took. Holly obediently slid up his lusty, firm body to his chest where he held her head over his heart, kissing the top of her hair.

His bent fingers stroked her cheek, his heart beating rapidly like hummingbirds while his other hand slowly traced the lines up and down her back, sending quivering sex quakes to her already excited gender.

She ached badly.

And using her words confessed, "I ache, and I'm tender, sore."

His comment couldn't have surprised her more.

"You see the difference between him and me. I keep you sore and you know it's me."

He slipped his hand up her thigh to rest on her sore and swollen lips and squeezed.

"This is mine."

She wanted to respond by wincing, but she was too stunned, to have a response.

How to react? But she understood the warning.

They lay there awhile, the touch of their fingertips doing their talking. She thought back to London. She'd repeated the same intimacy as with Kaine — never able to have enough of each other. The thought saddened her, remembering how these first few days became a natural part of growing closer to a man, the attraction extreme, unable to stay apart.

She smiled, thinking about her special time with Kaine. The same insatiable drive to long for him. Kaine ... what a magnificent lover he'd been. She closed her eyes and remembered her sweet, unpredictable lover. In a few days, she, and Kaine would fall into the sweet, loving, rhythm of unquenchable rediscovery. But until then she slept in the devil's bed.

When Luka regained his strength, he lifted her face to him, and she awaited his potent kiss that would set her ablaze. She pumped his mouth reverently thirsty for him.

Luka, the powerhouse, responded with mounting passion, pulling her into him. He pulled her tightly to him, attempting to steal her breath away forever. His long, lean legs, wrapped themselves around hers, and he moved on top of her.

She returned his affection, and her legs naturally separated, opening and placing herself direct in line to make burning love with him. She'd settle for traditional, no frills, just passionate, durable, unadulterated lust.

Luka slipped his arms under her knees and pulled them up close to his body. His body lay soft and supple between her legs, and he slowly rubbed his swelling manhood against her.

Her stomach tingled inside, and impatience, she demanded to have this man again. He continued to rub as he became so strong he might have once scared her ... but not anymore. She welcomed him, reaching down for him and guided him inside her. Her short breaths change into a pant in his ear.

"You're bloody hot, wet, and mine, Babe." He declared.

There it was again. Mine!

No time to reflect, his long golden threads draped across her face, and the aroma of Desert Rose filled her senses. She moved to kiss his neck, his chin, but mostly she wanted his wet expressive tongue. She wanted to touch his lips and suck on the lusciousness of them. She ordered him between breaths.

"Luka, love me, hard — harder."

He chuckled, "As you wish luv. Don't I always please you?"

"As only you can." Her words became the magic potion.

Luka entered her with one long thrust. He filled her quickly, and he loved her closely, sweetly. His powerful arms let go of her legs. Then his hands moved up behind her back to hold onto her shoulders, shoving his rigid strength into her as if bliss became his single destination and nothing would keep him from entering.

Luka moved in and out of her with ease, sweet, loving. Luka stayed with her, rocking and rocking. He stayed with her, filling her mouth with kisses, oh, so sweet kisses, and he stayed with her when her body shook beneath him, each quake giving everything up to him. He stayed with her and kissed her tear-stained cheeks because he loved her with his healing heart.

Her tears fell knowing that soon she would leave him.

"Never forget Babe," he whispered.

"... You belong to me."

Chapter Thirteen

DESPERADO

Holly stretched out long and languid, to erase the kinks in her muscles. Luka's passionate loving swallowed her whole. She turned over on her side to look into his peaceful, handsome face. Her hand instantly went to his cheek, where she lay stroking it, outlining his masculine features. She leaned in to kiss his neck and announced.

"I've got to get ready for Jaden."

"That doesn't sound right!" He joked as one eye rolled up like a window shade.

"But the fact remains, I must get beautiful for another man."

"Won't take long, stand up, my beauty."

"You're incorrigible Luka Hunter." She rebuked, kissing his nipple and nibbling on him a bit with her lips.

"Me? You're Miss Love in the afternoon!"

She smiled at him reminded how cute and cuddly he became after loving her.

"I do love the way you need me, by the way," he said.

Great! She had his attention and had fooled him.

Holly dragged herself from the warmth and protection of his embrace.

"Since I'm your lady, tell me your middle name."

Luka looked at her with a twinkle in his eyes, followed by a wrinkle pressing his forehead.

"My bloody middle name? Why?"

"It's a common American tradition. When people commit, we divulge the horrid middle names we would otherwise keep secret." She smiled hoping he'd taken her inquiry as a challenge.

"Tell yours first?"

"Easy. It's Anne."

"That's not awful. It's beautiful."

"Oh, but a few are."

Luka started to laugh. "I see you're one of the lucky ones."

"Okay, your turn."

He grew quiet.

Holly watched the afternoon sun reflecting off his sweaty body, the turquoise colored sheet barely covering his plump resting sex.

He mumbled.

"What?"

"My middle name. Hunter."

"Really? Then what's your last name?"

"You asked for my middle name. You have it. Forget that, my luv, we need to meet Jaden."

Holly wondered why he refrained from talking about being a Sinclare. But he would soon.

Holly strolled into the bathroom and looked out at the valley stretching long and beautiful. After a refreshing shower, she stepped out of the glass-enclosed shower to find Luka waiting.

"Sorry, Babe. I didn't want to join you if Jaden expected to see us any time earlier than after the sunset."

Holly laughed, she stepped out to dress, but on the way by, she kissed him. He teased, by pretending to pull her into the shower with him, but he playfully allowed her to escape. She turned to watch him stretch and lather his body while she dried off her legs.

"Luka, this location shot. If we shoot out by the pool, it becomes another cliché set. It's not a location. It's any pool USA. What if we take Jaden out to, maybe the stables, to saddle horses? Or we could sit on the rail of the corral fence, feed the horses hay, and then do our song? Or, we could even go for a walk in the desert out behind the yard. The cameras can follow capturing the silent beauty. We are out here in the middle of nowhere with all this quiet beauty. Would that be feasible?"

Silence.

Seconds later, Luka rinsed the last of the bubbles from his hair and body, turned off the shower, and quickly selected a towel on the way to the door.

"Where are you going?"

Luka kissed her rough and fast, sucking her bottom lip into his mouth. When he let go, he looked into her eyes with wonderment.

"Fucking brilliant idea! I have to call the camera crew. We need them here to check out the locations."

His words trailed him as he stood pressing buttons on his cellular. His hair hung dripping wet. While he waited for someone to answer, he pulled on fresh blue Levi's. He shot her another adoring look.

"That's another reason why I love you. You have

bloody brilliant ideas."

She took in the words slowly.

Why I love you.

Did Luka realize what he'd confessed? She hadn't heard those words since Friar Manor when he'd reluctantly confessed to being in love with her. A long time since he'd acknowledged with words that he loved her. Mister use-your-words. Oh, she'd known it for months, perhaps since the Hard Rock. But the words sounded beautiful though she wondered if he noticed.

Holly hadn't repeated her words of declaration to love him since the forced confession in L.A.

Someone answered his call, and Luka continued to do what he did best, setting up the next scene.

He pulled on a fresh, blue denim shirt and quickly rolled the sleeves up to his elbows ready to work. He sat on the edge of the bed, slipped on white socks, and then pulled on his rough out boots and stood as if a handsome character out of a Western movie. The bandit no doubt, getting ready to meet the outlaws at high noon. In this case, rock music outlaws from England.

He slipped on his wooly, sheep-lined vest on his way out the door issuing orders, pressing the phone to his ear, happiest when putting a deal together, well almost. She smiled realizing how his lavish attention contributed to her belief of his love then the inevitable sorrow to follow on the heels as it rushed to her heart.

He was not her man.

She would leave.

In a few more days, her man would come … for her.

Holly shook her head and turned her thoughts to

dressing for the interview with Jaden. The wardrobe girl brought her a few choices and left them in the closet. She wanted to reflect the softness of the Old West but protected from the crisp outdoors. What better way than a red-plaid, tailored, cowgirl-shirt, complete with a red neck scarf to compliment a soft, ankle length, dark-brown suede skirt, with a brown suede waistcoat and rawhide-colored cowboy boots? She fluffed her hair that hung halfway down her back, crinkled from the locks being braided. This surely must be a comfortable western look for hanging around the stables or strolling past cacti.

Holly thought to put in a pair of turquoise earrings when her finger bumped her diamond stud from Kaine. The image of Kaine popped into her mind giving her the precious diamond, as a gift of his commitment to her, drew a momentary sigh, then excitement.

Kaine should be on his way to her.

And then Holly wondered why Luka never asked her to take the diamond out of her ear.

Holly passed on the other earrings. For the first time, she put on camera make-up alone. And the thought of the diamond stud gave the ever-present Kaine the chance to fill her thoughts. But, not of joy and celebration of an impending reunion, no, instead the continual hatred of Sarah Cromwell flooded her thoughts, reminding her of makeup she'd put on to cover the beating she'd taken from that bitch down in that hell whole.

A warm thought replaced the ugly ones. Kaine was coming. The true meaning of his arrival flooded her, overwhelming her in the remaining moments. As usual, the ghost took a step back, but Kaine made his point. His memory lived strong in her heart, and the fact remained, ready or not, Kaine was coming. When she finished primping, she picked up the waist length, suede jacket that matched the skirt and then mineral water from the kitchen on her way out to find Luka scouting locations.

Holly discovered a beautiful afternoon in the desert with a cold, crisp, and biting winter breeze blowing gently, clearing the skies. The energy from the breeze brought her an exciting prediction of a productive day. As a new woman with her own show, she and her baby remained safe. She watched Luka scurrying about issuing orders. Then she joined in, and they checked the lights and marked the locations exactly where they would shoot.

Soon, excited voices descended upon her and turned to find a couple of women and a man flanking an outrageously, handsome, blonde-haired man. Holly recognized him from his picture, Jaden Moore. His hair straight, shoulder length, and more handsome in person than on the CD covers. Jaden's rock star image didn't follow him to the desert.

Jaden dressed casually, in an oatmeal colored, thermal shirt with a banded collar, and loose light blue Levi's, and a thick, tan leather jacket. He looked more like an executive on vacation than an internationally famous rock star.

From behind her, someone said.

"Jaden, fucking bloody great to see you mate."

And then Luka passed her, but not before, he'd taken the opportunity to slap her on the cheek of her derrière.

He loved that. She'd have to speak to him.

Luka continued over to Jaden and gave him a great big brotherly welcome. They stood chatting a moment, then Luka turned.

"Here she is, Miss Holly Hill. Holly, Jaden Moore. This chap and I go way back, too far back," he affirmed, laughing, his eyes flashing with the secrets he and Jaden shared.

"I could tell you stories." They elbowed each other in a howl of laughter.

Holly glanced at him, the sparkle in Luka's eyes shining brightly, enjoying his old friend again. And she marveled at the people that he called old friends.

Luka walked Jaden through a quick, dry rehearsal.

Holly handed Jaden a printout of her tentative inquiries.

"These are different from the usual track of questions," Jaden observed.

"Well, Luka wants me to strive to find unusual subjects. The format is as if two old friends bumped into each other out in the desert. That's the hook. It can be tricky since I met you, but I'd like to keep it light today, fun, looking for positive changes in the band, what you're looking forward to in the New Year. And always remember, we could end up on a different topic."

Jaden smiled, "Sounds easy enough."

"It is and here is the choice of songs I have learned. You decide which you want to close with Jaden."

Jaden selected her favorite.

Luka decided Holly would be outside in a corral, brushing down her horse when Jaden dropped by for a chat. They could talk while she fed and watered the horse, then stroll out the back to the desert to end up with them back at the corral fence. There they would sit, play acoustic guitars for the closing shot.

Jaden fulfill her prediction as a wonderful guest, and his

comments on his dislike of the cold, desert weather kept everyone in stitches. And, when Luka hadn't been watching, Jaden opened up to share with her while standing in the corral waiting for the camera to focus.

"I've never seen Luka with a woman. I mean, like you. He seems happy that's smashing. I'm glad for the both of you."

Holly didn't dare respond. He wouldn't be happy for long. She planned to leave him in three days. What she offered.

"Luka is a wonderful man."

When the interview ended, Jaden, warm and friendly, left to chat with the crew and signed a few autographs for them — another nice, charming, Englishman.

To that point, each of her guests was professional and polished. She'd been lucky. None of the stereotypical slob rock star she'd anticipated in the early days. But with the new locations that would be added, Holly turned her thoughts to discussing with Luka about adding more women to the interview line-up. Oh, but wait, soon she would leave him.

Jaden wandered off with the crew and his entourage following him. From behind, Luka took her by the arm, and he pulled her from her thoughts of abandonment to the opposite direction of the exiting crowd. He pushed her up against the wall of the barn, close, oh so close.

"Brilliant," he praised, as his breath blew hot on her face.

"Excellent as usual. I'm impressed with how you encouraged him to open up with that touching touring story. And when you leaned up against his upper arm like a close friend, well, you never forget what I tell you about personalizing. How do you do it? Come to me. Can I kiss the beautiful enchantress?"

"With you close to me, what else would I want to do with my handsome producer?"

He kissed her, and they allowed the potency of the kiss to force them down into the hay.

He laughed and broke the kiss. "If we don't stop, you can guess what will happen?"

"I look forward to it."

"Well, my luv, I'm embarrassed to say, I may have to have a lay down to keep up with your demands."

"Demands?" She challenged, laughing.

"Yes, rest, Miss Hill." He insisted with that twinkle in his eyes as he moved away from her. He stood and reached for her hand to help her up and then he picked the hay from her hair.

Then he stopped.

She saw it in his eyes.

He didn't have any restraint when it came to keeping any distance from her. He couldn't get enough of her. Luka leaned her against the stall and kissed her with no urgency.

Holly broke his kiss and pulled her fingers from his silky hair. "I need to catch my breath. Do you realize Mr. Hunter that you absolutely take my breath away?"

"I've been told a lot of things in my day, but not that Babe. I rather like having that effect on you."

"Well, it's more than that." And she wrapped her leg around his and rubbed her hips into his. Her hands dropped to hug his denim covered cheeks, pulling him into her as she looked up into his amazingly gorgeous eyes, knowing that one day soon she would never see them again.

"Well Poppa Bear, you're right about naps, time for me to get a bit of rest. With all the excitement and steady diet of loving you, I'll never make the concert tonight if I don't sleep."

Luka never stopped gazing into her eyes.

"Right, you need your rest." His hand dropped to the place where another's child grew.

"I have a few things I need to do. I'll come in and wake you when it's time. All right?"

Holly understood what Luka meant.

"I'm counting on it." Holly tiptoed up to kiss him and placed her hand on his rugged, unshaven face, his five o'clock shadow growing in a shade darker, making him sensual and attractive with his new cowboy image.

Holly pushed him away, lingering, holding his hand. She let go and headed toward the house, stopping beyond the barn doors. She turned and over her shoulder asked.

"Will you make me scream again?"

Her sexy lover looked at her with his cool blue eyes and vowed. "My reason to live is to please you, Babe. You can count on it."

Chapter Fourteen

WHO'S CRYING NOW

Holly lay asleep almost as if comatose. Pure determination compelled her dark-haired dream lover to slip in for a visit. Kaine would do what he needed to keep her from Luka.

He sat close to her.

His magnificent face filled with concern, his dark, blue eyes telling her something she couldn't understand. Kaine's face came close to hers, his cheek rubbed hers, and his breath blew on her ear. So close, his sweet and familiar scent engulfed her.

Holly smiled because she'd missed him. She moved her head to place her lips on his.

He waited.

His lips brushed hers and then pulled away allowing his words flowed.

"Wait for me. I love you. I'll be here soon."

She'd expected Kaine to come to her this afternoon. Kaine, strong, virile and loving, refusing to share her.

And Luka knew.

Her hand instinctively went to her waist. There in her

exhausted slumber, she found Luka's flesh and blood hand tight around her waist pulling her back from Kaine, to fill in the length of his body. His soft lips pressed lightly against her forehead to reminding her of his presence too. Luka must have thought she lay asleep because the scent of his breath rode the words of his whisper.

"My feelings are deep for you, my love, and they scare me. I hope I never let you down, Babe."

His sweet words fell on a heart that belonged to another. Holly tried to return to the dreamtime, but too late for another reunion with Kaine. The freshness of his memory no longer swirled in her dream mind. The taste of Kaine lost in a misty shadow.

However, the message remained clear.

Kaine would arrive in four days prepared to take her with him, and she couldn't move to wipe the tears dripping from her eyes.

Luka faced her and snuggled in closer, his top hand securely around her. His body heat warmed her and then blew hotter until she lay engulfed by the heat storm.

Holly cracked an eyelid to discover an inky darkness. She'd slept through the last of the afternoon. The moonlight cut into the nightfall and allowed one silver bar of light to stream in the room.

Luka's body molded to hers, and he pushed against her stomach, hard, wanting her, but he wouldn't dare wake her for his pleasure.

He became the thoughtful gentleman once again.

Holly peeked up to see Luka breathing softly, resting peacefully, his long hair covering parts of his amazing face like a golden curtain. He simply took her breath away.

Memories of long ago in London swirled in her mind of and another nap when Kaine returned from the sound check. How he'd been out of control from the cocaine and whiskey. He'd taken her with a frightening strength she would have never thought possible. And from those agonizing moments of confusion, they'd conceived this child.

Kaine apologized, explaining how she'd been irresistible. How he'd thought of her to the point of lousing up the sound check at Wembley Stadium. But Kaine's sweetness soon filled her forgiving heart. And she carried the fruit of his strong, sexual desire for her growing inside her.

How different this nap, with the never satiable Luka but glad she didn't need to submit to another long session with him. She laid relaxed on the pillow content to soak in the gorgeous sight of him doused in the silvery moonlight.

Without opening his eyes, his hand started slowly to roam her back.

Holly mirrored his movements by sliding her hand over his soft denim cowboy shirt to his hot neck. She scooted upwards under his arm, coming close to his face and leaned into his full lips, chapped from the cool Arizona breeze. She captured his full bottom lip, sucked it into her mouth easily, lovingly, and then pressed her mouth full on his.

Luka opened his mouth and softly, sweetly kissed her, pulling her closer to him and then under him. Luka wrapped his arm around her and then threw his leg over her as if to swallow her alive.

Holly laid kissing Luka until time didn't matter. She tasted his love, content to have his arms embracing her, his leg wrapped around hers, his hair woven with hers, his body heating hers.

"Luka," she murmured into his lips after a long, long while. But she never spoke of any love for him.

"Hummmmmm." She allowed and then whispered.

"When do we need to leave for the concert?" She asked between long-drawn-out kisses.

"Too soon," he whispered in return.

Chapter Fifteen

HAVE YOU EVER NEEDED SOMEONE SO BAD?

Holly laid with Luka in his strong, loving arms for what seemed like hours. Luka leaned his warm body into hers and whispered in her ear.

"We got to get up, Babe." His breath sent waves of tingling shivers up and down her skin.

"We've pushed the envelope and don't have much time."

Time.

Luka promised they had the gift of time, yet what happened to it? They always needed to be somewhere, to be there in a few minutes. Holly shook the thoughts from her mind and reluctantly rolled over and swung her feet to the carpet.

She'd already forgotten Luka and his warm, comfortable embrace and headed for the wardrobe stocked with costume choices for the shoot, unsure what to select for her evening's outfit. She chose a long-sleeved, three-quarter length, copper colored-suede dress, with fawn colored piping and matching doeskin boots. She added a crème colored fringed waistcoat, chocolate colored Stetson and then set them on the bed.

Holly joined Luka in the bathroom, delighting in the shared closeness of them performing the simple list of personal hygiene routines, brushing their teeth and washing their faces together. Holly put on mascara, ran a plump blush brush of a soft bronze color across the high ridges of her cheekbones. She ran a glossy finger pad across her lips and sprayed a dab of Joy perfume behind her ears and at each pulse point on her wrist.

Luka smiled. "You're intending on driving me bloody out of my mind?"

"My life's goal!"

He smiled again. "I never dreamed it would be this bloody great to be with one lady, day after day. I never dared to believe happiness waited for me, Babe. You've made it all possible."

"And how is that?"

"By giving me the greatest gift of all. Trust."

"Trust? Why wouldn't I trust you at this point?"

Let me count the ways, she thought.

"Many long, old reasons and none you should be told."

Holly watched his eyes glaze over dismissing his private crimes, done with talking, his confession surprising her again. What ate at Luka Hunter Sinclare? What other plots hatched that made him believe himself to be untrustworthy, and unlovable? So terrible, that everyone agreed with that assessment.

Luka brushed out his, long blonde angel hair and wrapped a blue headscarf across his forehead. He changed into a fresh blue-denim shirt and Levi's.

The effect on his baby blues dazzled her, and she followed him out into the bedroom, grabbed her Stetson and fringed waistcoat, and glided down the long, spiral staircase.

Luka picked up his sheepskin-lined coat hanging on the entrance hall tree and beige Stetson. He joined her at the doorway.

Once inside the Jeep, Luka pressed the pedal to the floor, spraying rocks and gravel behind them, as they headed toward the Tucson Arena.

Luka quickly whipped through a fast food restaurant. They'd both laughed at his dinner choice. But even funnier when he pulled out a hundred-dollar bill and couldn't pay for it.

Holly quickly scrambled in her purse for the cash and teased.

"You're one classy dude."

Later, they sat in the Jeep stuffing the hamburgers in their mouths, washing down their fries with good old sugar based soda. They continued laughing at the sight of Luka eating junk food!

They walked with lightning speed toward the backstage entrance. Luka gave his name for two *all-access laminates* and clipped them to their coats. Holly slipped her hand into Luka's, and he led her to the band's dressing room located under the stage.

She noticed the unusual crowd. She remembered *Hurrikaine* backstage at Wembley Stadium in London. There they all looked like music outlaws, scary and intimidating. But not here, instead, there stood an array of bare-chested and naked women. Others strutted around as if nothing out of the ordinary. The heat of judgment and embarrassment lash at Holly's cheeks and Luka must have sensed it flow freely from her hand into his because he asked to be taken somewhere else.

They stood in a large area where lounge chairs and buffet tables lined the wall. Holly gathered two mineral waters for herself, Luka, trying to understand why a woman would demean herself, shocked by what she'd witnessed, and exactly what life out on the road truly meant.

No wonder Luka said sex was plentiful and thrown in his face. She saw how different she'd been indeed! Those women debased themselves, displaying their wares for the picking. The rock star's life was seriously decadent and more disgusting than she'd ever imagined.

Luka leaned in laughing with a few members of the band that escaped the gangs of women while she drained her water. She smiled watching Luka, what a piece of work. She'd learned many important business and communication skills from simply watching him.

Once again, Luka turned to Holly with a giant smile. Must be something happening.

"We've been invited to an informal gathering at a local cantina after the show. Want to go?"

She could tell from his tone of voice, he did and expected her to agree and follow him anywhere.

"Sounds like fun."

Luka stopped to visit with an unfamiliar man. Holly watched the man become entranced with Luka as she did long ago in London. Of course, she'd never believed, she met the man that would ask her to marry him that fateful day on the street in Chelsea, moments after she arrived in

London. The spell lasted for a day and then she met the man of her dreams — Kaine — surprise!

Holly loved when Luka turned to look at her. The familiar glow would arrive whenever he did, showing her his happiness by taking her into his world, introducing her to anyone near him.

She reacted warmly to most people, she liked people, but Luka was the type of personality that never met a stranger. The ease and comfort he displayed with people she deemed uncanny. She shivered when she saw him heading for her, flanked by a tall, nice looking dark-haired cowboy.

"Holly this is Marty. He's with the local radio station and saw a broadcast of HHW. He wants the local affiliate to add your show."

Holly understood her role. Woo, this man as a business opportunity. Holly extended her hand.

"Marty, how nice to meet you."

"Miss Hill, I'm a big fan of your show. I understand from Luka, you interviewed the band today?"

"Yes, please, call me Holly, and yes, it should air the first of the year?" She shot a questioning glance to Luka to confirm.

"Yeah, Marty, you're going to the jam session at the cantina later?"

"Wouldn't miss it, Luka. I'll save you and Holly seats. I have a reserved table down front. The place will be jammed with local color and the A-list of out-of-town concert visitors here tonight."

Holly watched Marty trying to impress Luka with his clout. Everyone wanted to please Luka as she did. But Luka never heard it. He always expected the best treatment.

Luka smiled at her, pulling her to his side saying to Marty. "See you there mate." And he graced Marty with one of his sunny Luka smiles.

"Great!" Marty confirmed as his attention diverted to someone hollering for him.

Luka took Holly's hand and led her out onto the floor of the arena. They walked up a couple of rows until even with the stage and found their complimentary seats located in an exclusive section close to the theater-in-the-round. Seconds later, the lights went down, and the roar of the crowd went up in a flash.

Holly watched *Bon Jour* perform for the first time. Two and a half rocking hours later, Holly stood with Luka in the parking lot waiting for the valet to bring their Jeep while her body relaxed and unwound from the sensory explosion the music caused. She pulled her earplugs out reminiscing about when Jaden came right over to their section and pointed right at them creating a moment and special thrill.

Luka held her hand, repeatedly squeezing it, and she considered he realized it too. Clearly, his anxiety focused on the action at the cantina than at the concert. Finally, the valet returned with the Jeep, and they set off in search of their late night's pleasure, the rockin' concert already forgotten. She listened to the local station pumping out the bands tunes to pay homage to the evening.

Luka hollered. "I've found it! The cantina. I hate to admit it, but I can bloody well find my way around the world easier than I can when I'm behind the wheel with a map. I can tell you. It didn't look bloody good for a while."

They laughed heartily at his limitation.

And there weren't too many, she silently thought.

Luka pulled up to a lively Mexican restaurant, the parking lot filled with four-wheeled drive vehicles and pickup trucks. It took a bit of time, apparently more than he wanted to find a parking space. He seemed in a hurry.

Luka spewed a stream of curse words, turned and reminded Holly.

"It is a good idea if you chat up Marty a bit. Circulate and meet a few of the affiliates here. What do you think?"

And she remembered Kaine's words, at her hotel in London.

You'll find what I think means little. Luka runs the show. I'm the king pawn to move about where needed.

How true, and she and placed a hand gently upon his warm cheek, ready with the perfect answer.

"I should do what my manager thinks I should do. But I will miss my lover if this takes me away from him for too long."

Luka leaned over and kissed Holly. His hands pulled her to his chest, even though, the resistance of her seat belt cut her across her upper torso. She never said a word because Luka would kiss her to Oblivion.

Being restricted, seemed to bother Luka. He jumped out and hurried around to help Holly out of her side of the Jeep. He lifted her up and let her slowly slide down the front of him. When her face paralleled him, he saw her pain and quickly asked.

"What? Babe, are you okay?"

"It's nothing, a twinge in my ribs."

She'd lied.

She'd remembered the first time Kaine held her up at the Hard Rock and let her slide down the front of his body. The memory quickly invaded her when her defenses drained to low.

How unfair of Kaine.

The memory ignited her, becoming too real. She needed to stop, and then like magic, Luka pressed his lips to hers to snap her back to him.

He knew.

His sweet, moist, passionate lips called her to the present. He'd made the vivid memory vanish as he set her down, took her hand, and placed it in the crook of his arm.

But the faded memory started fighting to make its presence known.

Holly forced herself to look up to Luka, praying he didn't see Kaine in her eyes.

And at that moment, she thought Kaine might have more of a fight on his hands due to Luka's overwhelming adoration for her.

He patted her hand as if he understood.

But he didn't.

Luka had done everything in his power to make the suffering and the pain vanish and bring her happiness. Yet Kaine lingered under her skin, in her heart and she wondered if a memory could quickly derail her, what would she do when she laid eyes on Kaine?

Yes, Kaine was coming for her.

Chapter Sixteen

I WANT TO SPEND MY LIFETIME LOVING YOU

Holly's betraying thoughts fled as the sounds of laughter leaked from the doorway when Luka gave their names at the private entertainer's entrance.

The bouncer escorted Luka and Holly into a small, smoky room that held less than one hundred people, on a good night, but tonight it easily held twice that creating a fire hazard. He led them over to a ringside table where Marty sat nursing a draft beer. His face lit up when he saw Luka pulling out a chair for Holly.

"Luka, please, sit. What are you drinking?" The lanky man asked.

Luka leaned in and ordered and the den of the boisterous, crowd made it difficult to understand his words. During the next half hour, Marty introduced many people to Holly, the names and faces became blurred. When her mineral water arrived, she wished she'd asked for something much stronger to drink. She longed for a couple of sips of alcohol to take off the edge. She leaned over to taste of

Luka's Margarita. To her surprise, it contained none of the expected Tequila in it, hummm, curious. She must ask him later why he never drank alcohol. In this day of health consciousness, she accepted why he didn't smoke cigarettes, and he'd told her he no longer did drugs.

Luka, such a contradiction of terms to the whole rocker image or the customary vices associated with rock music. What a mysterious man.

The rack of stage lights flooded the small stage set up in front of Luka and Holly. From every direction, musicians descended upon the stage picking up their resting instruments to tune and then magnetically formed a huddle. The lead guitarist broke from the gathering and walked up to the microphone.

"It's true, all the rumors. We have visitors from out-of-state sitting in on this set." As he finished his introduction, the concert headliners stepped up onto the stage, looking refreshed and excited, not as if they'd finished a grueling two-hour set.

The crowd went wild. The English visitors strapped on their instruments ready for something to happen. Jaden, the lead singer, walked up to the microphone and in his cool casual manner, started a personable dialog with the audience, as during the concert.

Jaden's charming demeanor made her comfortable as if she sat at a gathering of old friends. He then stoked her curiosity with his short introduction.

"I'd like to get a big round of applause for an old mate of mine. We started out together many years ago. And tonight I'd like him to come up and start this set off with a song he wrote, "One Love." Come on, he needs encouragement. Let's get Luka Hunter up here."

Holly turned to Luka, with her eyebrows frozen upward pushing into her forehead. She saw Luka equally taken aback by the outrageous request.

The longer Luka sat stunned, grinning at the singer, giving him the old 'what the fuck did you want to go and do that for?' look, the louder the crowd stomped their feet and whistled.

They demanded Luka, and it would take Luka to quiet them. Luka finally stood up, tying his long, luscious hair back with the blue bandanna around his forehead. He instantly looked like a rock star. Why had she never noticed that?

The crowd continued to whistle and holler while stomping their feet even louder.

Luka surveyed the room as he stood straight and tall, his face registering complete amazement. Then he turned and looked down to Holly.

"See how you bring me luck, Babe? " One Love" is for you."

Luka reached out and squeezed her hand meaningfully. He forced a broad smile as if to encourage himself to take the stage. His expression said he wondered what would happen next.

Reeling from the information that Luka sang, made her wonder how many more secrets did he have? Of course, he'd written the number one love ballad of all time, "One Love" but that tidbit didn't answer any of the questions that ran circles in her mind … Luka could sing?

Holly watched Luka select a beautiful electric guitar and then slipped the leather strap over his head. He adjusted the guitar. The all too familiar feeling arrived of watching her man get ready to perform. He played guitar too — another surprise.

She understood why Kaine's performance at Friar Manor, singing "My Lady" for her, never impressed Luka. Because he could do the same, write her a hit song and sing it.

As usual, seeing Luka ready to entertain the crowd sent a potent aphrodisiac running through her body. She watched him carefully run the pick over the strings and her stomach flipped with butterflies. Luka could play the guitar, Luka could do anything ... except stop Kaine from coming after her.

The band started up the familiar, multi-platinum tune made world famous by *Hurrikaine*, more importantly with Kaine's one of a kind voice. And for a split second Luka hesitated, seemingly overwhelmed, and looked out into the audience. His vulnerabilities passed over his countenance, an uncommon occurrence to Luka Hunter.

Holly watched his eyes search the crowd until they stopped and locked on hers. She stared back, and the flashing blue eyes of Luka, the singer, blew her away.

Luka smiled that sexy boyish smile, she'd loved since the first days with his gleaming teeth.

He flicked his long bewitching hair back behind his shoulders, and there on the stage stood the gorgeous and sexy Luka Hunter. The stage lights started to dim, centering one single light on him. It made him appear more handsome than imagined. His usually cool, even-toned voice trembled at first and then gained strength as he continued.

"Ladies and gentlemen, against my better judgment, I'm

going to sing with these fuckers."

The crowd broke into a roar of camaraderie.

Luka smiled even bigger.

She relished the pure joy blast from his eyes.

"I wrote this song many, many years ago. But it's been recent that I've found new meaning. I'd like to dedicate this song to a special lady."

Luka turned his back to the crowd and hit the first chord. He took another step and hit the next chord louder on the guitar, and the sound ripped through the tiny room. He whirled around and with one-step, closed the distance between him and the microphone. He faced the crowd, as the single golden spotlight, drenched the man with the angel-eyes. He started to sing with a bluesy, commanding voice. A smooth, smoky, sexy, blues man's voice.

A seductive voice Holly would have never predicted.

The pale spotlight fell gently, softly, like a ray of light from above, drenching his face, highlighting his trim, firm body as he swayed his hips in sync with his guitar. And his voice rang out — beautiful, soft, rich, and melodic. The band joined in harmonizing as if they'd been in constant rehearsals. At the break in the song, Luka stepped back and winked at Holly apparently enjoying how blown away she looked.

Luka could sing.

And how could he sing!

Holly could barely stay in her seat. Everyone clapped and bobbed their heads and women of all ages were up dancing.

Luka Hunter.

Wow, he burned up the guitar with chops he'd

obviously kept up, but when did he have the time? When he slung his guitar over his back and stepped back up to the microphone, his legs parted, his eyes closed as he belted out one familiar lyric after the other as a professional.

Holly couldn't tell, due to Luka's riveting performance, how much time elapsed since he'd left the stage. He stood lit up and the fire in his eyes glowed so real, so astonishingly real. Luka remained and played one song after the other until the end of the set. Luka and the band jammed and tore the house down covering blues songs.

The band relied on familiar crowd control techniques to stir up the crowd. Luka joined Jaden in duets and didn't disappoint. The frenzied crowd released recurring explosions of crazy applause realizing they'd been privy to a special moment that would go down in music history.

The audience refused to allow to Luka leave the stage. Eventually, the applause died down so the band could close the show with one final song without Luka.

Luka stepped off the stage and slipped in beside Holly. His hand shook, and a sheepish humility washed over his face as he strained to catch his breath. His hand dropped to her thigh where he fanned his trembling fingers to steady himself. He pulled her near him.

Holly, taken aback by Luka's insecurity, felt special because Luka needed someone, and for once, she filled the bill. Holly proudly placed her arm around his neck and leaned on his shoulder.

He kissed her ear and confirmed.

"You've changed my life, Babe."

Flattered of course, but she'd nothing to do with this and changed the subject.

"Is there anything you haven't done?" She whispered loudly into his tiny ear with the golden hoop earring as her free hand wiped the sheen away from his neck with a cocktail napkin. Then she inconspicuously kissed his neck, running up to the tip of his earlobe.

Luka turned to her, so close, ran his tongue along her lips, and then up into her hair, finding her ear.

"Today, I didn't make you scream...."

Chapter Seventeen

STAR STAR

Holly sat faced with a difficult situation trying to reconcile the bluesman that held her, and then the angel eyed CMT executive. What does one say to her lover when she discovers he should have become the singing sensation instead of Kaine?

The moment seemed awkward.

What to say to Luka?

She'd seen another facet of his constantly changing persona. She needed to admit, there was no end to his talents and abilities.

She'd learned a lot during the past two days. She'd discovered a kinder, gentler Luka. Distanced from his numerous critics he'd changed. Even Luka pointed out the years mellowed Kaine, a usually hard-hearted womanizer. It would seem they also softened Luka's harsh edges, not that she'd excused the London production. But Luka, the inflexible, ruthless businessman, and Luka, the lover, two different men. Due to his intense feelings, he'd demanded from himself, that he hide his sweet, vulnerable side. She'd spent four months with him, learning his ways, the limits, if any to his inexhaustible creativity and the pain. But oh so much pleasure, and through it all, his eyes long-established — that he adored her.

However, Kaine, truly equally dynamic, proved his abilities in four short days and those hours burned in her memory and heart with no rival even with all the time spent with Luka. Would Luka simply have vanished if she'd spent three months with Kaine? Would Luka have become the small blip on the radar, long forgotten?

No reason to wonder.

Kaine was on his way.

Kaine may be in transit at that moment on his way back to her. What messages were sent these past two days to her believing she accepted the rest of his intentions? Did it matter? He'd forgiven her, he loved her, he missed her, and he planned to come and get her.

The problem, she wasn't there.

She sat here, placating Luka until his arrival.

Holly sat stunned, lost in thought long after the cantina closed, sitting with Luka and *Bon Jour* swapping road stories. Naturally, the fans interrupted, stopping by, to congratulate the bands return to touring. Others offered congratulations to Luka for his show-stopping performance.

It had been a magical night, and she wore her pride for Luka and counted herself lucky to have witnessed him. She filled with sadness when the party finally decided to end.

Outside the cantina, in the cold, crisp Arizona desert air, Luka took Holly into his warm embrace. He leaned her up against the Jeep and kissed her as if he possessed a fire raging inside him. A firestorm she recognized as the fiery passion after performing on the stage. And all she could think to herself, what was it with musicians and the lust for sex after performing?

As if, he'd read her mind.

"I can't bloody wait to get you back to bed!" His breath was hot and insistent before he tore out of the parking lot burning rubber.

Holly welcomed the long, long night ahead but worried about Luka's loving her with his best as she imagined how hot his flames of desire burned.

He jumped out of the Jeep, barely parked in the driveway, and took her hand to hurry up the stairs, tearing her clothes from her body. After he'd left a trail of his shirt, vest, and pants, Luka seized her and fell with her upon the huge king-sized bed, laughing, rolling head overhead with her with no formalities.

Luka's feverish kisses told her how quickly he would take her. She rapidly separated her legs to show him her swift surrender. One firm push in, and he pushed faster and faster, his body broke out in sweat. She slid her hands up his damp back, to his shoulders where she held on, pulling him, receiving all of him.

Luka fucked her with a passion she'd yet to meet, and he moved fast, then faster, too fast to be believed. Harder and harder he moved, squirming and thrusting. His excited pant in her ear, his hot words of love and desire turned her on more than she wanted, and his wet mouth searched for hers until it arrived. His tongue dipped in, he took her with a fury. His movements became sharp, short, and deliberate. He pulled himself almost out of her, allowing the tip to penetrate, driving her crazy from wanting all of him. All the while pleasured sounds trickled from his throat, betraying him with sounds of satisfaction. One long, final thrust drove him to the other side of Oblivion that he'd sought deep inside her, and froze, his sexy voice filled her ear with words of commitment and a wonderful future. Then he collapsed on her, moans of satisfaction flowed freely.

Luka relaxed and wrapped Holly with his body as he dropped beads of sweat all over her flesh while his body continued to quake with irregular tremors.

Holly planted a trail of kisses from his chest to his lips.

"Well." She whimpered, "We've got to put you on the stage more often."

Her tone was more playful than serious. But what an inspired lover he'd become. What a great, sexual, power surge. Somehow, the music connected, resonating inside of Luka creating a powerful, electrical surge that continued to emanate from him.

Time ceased to matter to either of them. Finally, when Luka calmed his breath, he nibbled at her ear reminding her of his return.

"I'm sorry Babe. Forgive me, I couldn't wait for you."

"I see," she said, swallowing a teasing laugh and added.

"You're absolutely fabulous. But, look who did the screaming."

He laughed good-naturedly. "Okay! Okay, but remember, little lady, I've barely warmed up, I'm ready for more."

"Oh, I'm counting on that," she challenged.

Holly rolled over and out the side of the bed before he could catch her. Thirsty, she wandered downstairs for a cup of herbal tea. And a much needed moment to gain her balance. This sudden twist with Luka threw her off balance like being with a familiar stranger but stranger, nonetheless.

Who the hell was Luka Hunter Sinclare, the songwriter, the guitar player, the singer, and the bluesman? And don't forget entertainer.

Holly looked over her shoulder to find he'd followed her lead, but he walked with the quietness of a panther ready to catch his prey off guard.

"Hungry?" He asked.

Holly walked over to his naked body and her fingertips sprinted up his thigh to his sex. She caressed the length of his body, watching him close his eyes, accepting the strokes of her affection.

"Not yet. I'd rather spend my time making you happy."

She watched her words affect him, causing him to suck in a deep breath. The passion and fire between them never seemed to cool below hot and intense.

Luka leaned to press his succulent, chapped lips, pink from obsessively kissing her.

She pulled away to set the kettle on, then turned and opened the refrigerator.

"Have I scared you, Holly?"

He'd used her name, and his voice was laced with a fearful edge she'd never heard from the always confident Luka. She selected a carton of vanilla yogurt and a plump green apple. Then she remembered her question from the cantina. She ignored his inquiry, in favor for her own and turning to face him.

"Why don't you drink alcohol?" She asked as she popped the cap off the yogurt.

Luka flicked back a lock of his hair, held captive by the blue bandanna. He smiled generously. He took the container from her hand, dipped a stray spoon in it, and took a bite. He turned his back and leaned against the counter, his resting bulge threatening to capture her eyes for the rest of the conversation.

Holly blinked, to clear her thoughts and looked up to search his face.

Luka looked away from the corner of his eyes.

"I used to get too fucked up to remember details and in my line of work, I have to account for everything that is happening. A million little things can add up quickly. After one too many blackouts, I finally decided no more."

"You make it sound simple, to quit drinking."

"Essentially, it was. My father died of liver failure, alone in hospital. A few months before I decided enough was enough. I wasn't keen to follow his example. Cleanup became the answer — the decisions not that bloody difficult."

"Did you do it on your own?"

"You're asking ... did I check into rehab?"

"Sort of ..."

He interrupted, "No, a private surgeon detox me and then I talked with a psychoanalyst for a while. We went into the deep stuff because my addictions included both alcohol and cocaine and I was too far gone to stop cold turkey. I won't lie. It's bloody challenging sometimes. I have to take it one day at a time like all chemically depended addicts."

He took a breath.

Always in control.

Yet Luka Hunter hid a serious weakness.

A vice.

And to his credit in the insane world of rock music, he'd

remained clean and sober. How horrible of Kaine to tempt Luka by asking him to supply the cocaine in London.

"How long have you been clean and sober?"

"Little over six years."

"You stopped after you married Tessa?"

"Yes," he confirmed, then burst into a loud, sarcastic laugh as if realizing.

"What a bloody sobering experience she was."

"Doesn't it bother you when other people have a drink around you, or like when I did the cocaine in London?"

"There are moments like I said, but I try to think of it like I don't eat pumpkin pie, but it doesn't bother me if someone else does. Although, I do hate to be around drunks," he volunteered as he rolled his eyes. "Drunks, especially women drunks, they bother me."

Holly leaned against him.

Between bites of yogurt, his hand started to stroke her rounded belly. "Don't worry my beauty. There's nothing you could do to turn me away from you Babe."

Holly looked up into his beautiful face and then glanced down wondering how he could stand there casually, with his sex screaming for her to love him.

How lusty he looked wearing the bandanna, his long blonde angel locks draped over his shoulders and the gold medallion hanging from his neck.

His inviting demeanor compelled her to drop the carton of yogurt and wrap her arms around him, holding him close, oh so close. And then in a soft low tone, she dared to ask.

"Why don't you return to the stage, Luka Hunter? You belong there."

Luka pulled his head up, leaning an inch from her. This

move allowed her a complete view of his perfectly shaped body, with his hair hanging. He could add centerfold to his long list of accomplishments. He looked spectacular enough to be Man of the Century!

Luka's eyelids lowered casting an erotic aura over him.

At that moment, she surprised herself, dropping her plan to move away from the sexy Mr. Hunter and instead wanted to make nasty love with him, soon. He looked amazing, and a glance from him lured her in, inviting her to do with him as she pleased. And all that he'd said with his big baby blue eyes. His answer sent chills up and down her back and then straight to the fire burning below her belly.

In a husky, gravelly voice, Luka affirmed.

"You're good for me, Babe. When you say things like that, you make me believe I could do it again. There have been times in the past I've wished I could."

"I don't see why you can't? You have the money and connections. Hell, you own shares of CMT. You have a studio at the Dream compound. You have the ability and energy to promote yourself. And it's clear you have the talent to write and produce songs, a-n-d play them."

Holly moved slightly, pressing against him.

"You certainly have the body and looks as well as stage presence to become a top act."

Luka wrapped her unclothed flesh in his arms, and he looked down at her. His eyes said they pondered what to say. He watched her breath grow deeper.

Holly saw his hand rising in her peripheral vision until his fingertips traced her breast.

Luka outlined the hardening nipple, rapidly sending quivering little quakes throughout her body. She forgot her plan because he reminded her how much she enjoyed his touch.

Luka stood, quiet, thinking. Then he took his other hand and mirrored his movements until satisfied he'd aroused both nipples, cupping, massaging, and rubbing until he broke his silence.

"Let's take a few appetizers, mineral waters, and herbal tea upstairs. We'll fill the whirlpool, and I'll tell you all about when I was a rock star."

Chapter Eighteen

IT'S ONLY ROCK AND ROLL

Luka Hunter couldn't have surprised her more.

"You? A rock star?"

He paused, laughing at his self-proclaimed fame. He charmed her, even more, when he blew into her ear softly saying, "And when I'm finished, Miss Hill, I'm going to make you scream until the sun rises."

Holly looked into his eyes, those blue eyes to-die-for, and said, "Promise?"

"I'll make you scream." He guaranteed her in an even tone then turned and selected mugs and snacks.

Holly quickly searched the pantry for a tray, set a couple of tea bags on the tray, and turned to find a giant pile of goodies.

Holly laughed and joked. "Do you think there's enough here? I hope this holds us for a while!"

"Smashing, I don't want any reason to leave you."

"You're not serious about making love until sunrise?"

"I have no intention of watching the sunrise. My eyes will be on you, My Lady."

My Lady?

Luka called her by Kaine's pet name.

Unacceptable.

Luka could not do this. That's between she and Kaine. How could he mention it? Especially, when he expressed his evening's romantic intentions?

Another day, she thought.

I'll ask him not to call me that, another day.

Luka's firm hand followed her curves to where he stopped and started moving about her derrière in long stroking motions, breaking her train of thought.

"Something wrong?" He queried.

And she watched him wrinkle his forehead with concern.

"No. What could be wrong?"

Holly followed Luka up the winding staircase. She couldn't help to compare how Kaine and Luka treated her same. With one exception, with Luka, thus far, no temper tantrums.

And the most important fact, she'd spent four long months with Luka, instead of four short romantic days with Kaine. Then her attention focused on his naked, firm, cheeks, tucked neatly between his slim hips. His Malibu suntan lines almost faded, delighted her and the fantasy became too delicious in her mind.

His porcelain-skinned cheeks became a target inviting her hand to grab at him and tease. Holly laughed as she scooted close behind Luka. She continually grabbed at his flesh trying to make him spill the mountainous snack tray.

"Stop." Luka finally insisted.

"You're going to make me bloody well drop this." He stopped on the staircase, trying to balance the toppling tray and then hurried to the tiled area surrounding the large coral spa tub.

The midnight view overlooked the Tucson Valley. The stars danced with a clear full moon that hung high in the vast desert sky while the patchwork of dotted city lights twinkled.

Luka turned the bathroom dimmer switch to low, adjusted the piped-in blues CD, and then bent to turn on the faucet when he remembered her nearness to him. Tired of the game, he implored of her slightly irritated.

"Babe, please don't. I want to run the water."

Holly understood her teasing went far enough but astonished to learn there are limits and even boundaries with Luka. However, part of the trick was to recognize them.

"As you wish," she agreed, bending to kiss his left shoulder, where she noticed a thumb sized birthmark. She flashed back to him sitting in front of the Christmas tree and remembered she'd seen it then. But then the steamy, fragrant tub called her to come, soak and relax.

"I can't wait to submerge in those bubbles. I'm exhausted and worn out by your voracious love."

Her words true, Luka Hunter, proved to be a fiercely attentive lover. But what else would she have expected from him? She slid into the hot, fragrant bubbled water. Water that shot her straight into the arms of Kaine.

A vivid memory at Briarwood Castle exploded in her mind. Frighten her face would instantly betray her, especially with the barrage of traitorous thoughts that sought her immediate attention, she quickly looked to Luka.

For a fleeting flash, she saw Kaine instead in her mind. He headed straight for her, floating in the water, parting the bubbles. His hands glided up her bath oiled legs, to her private place where he plunged his finger deep inside her, sending bolts of electricity to excite her.

She closed her eyes to guard her secret and to keep the image of Kaine clear and focused. She parted her legs as his hand slipped around to her lower back pulling her into him. Her body captivated, his face moved near her with the clear scent of peppermint smothering her sense of smell. Confusion swept over her, forcing her eyes open, trying to distinguish this man. He licked his lips, preparing to kiss her.

He moved close, oh, so close.

Luka.

Luka's nimble fingers continued to penetrate her, gently, and then deliberately, knowing what would make her happy. He continued to kiss her feverishly, probing her mouth until ready for anything Luka offered. He positioned his fingertip on her pulsating bud, staying with her until she squirmed in his arms with ignited pleasure, unable to stop from dragging her nails down his back.

Holly forced opened her eyelids, breathless, enjoying every wave of her release. She pulled from Luka's mouth to ask between heaving breaths.

"What the hell happened, Papa Bear? Is that something you learned on the road?"

"Sort of ... but it's more about my desire when I'm with you. And besides, I owed you one."

"You still do. You didn't make me scream." She kissed him.

Pulling away from her, Luka glowed with a glint of promise in his sweet blue eyes. "I will."

Holly rested in his arms. Her mind raced of dreams, mostly of how he would keep his promise.

They sat in the warm, soothing water while his hand stroked her skin. Occasionally, he would turn on the whirlpool jets to massage a tender section of their muscles. Other times he bobbed his head to keep the beat to the soulful music.

"Luka, how do you know how to do the right thing to love me?"

He smiled, and half chuckled. "Well, I love sex. I love all the pleasures. But with you, I would say most is from experience, especially from what I learned while touring in Asia. How are you different? I would suppose the love and then mix in a bit of intuitiveness I hope will please you."

Apparently, she'd gotten as close to a confession of love as she would get for the moment. But as soon as the confession faded, the sting of blood rushed to her cheeks.

"You've been in love with a lot of women?"

"One … Carrin. I told you in London. Her deranged boyfriend came back into her life — she left me, and that's all there is to tell." Luka closed down again.

Holly needed to keep him open for her to learn what damaged him.

"I'm sorry. I do realize that talking about her distresses you. I didn't mean to open old wounds," she offered with sincerity.

"It's me. You have a right to know. That time in my life was fucked up, and I swore I would never fall in love again. That's why you're such a bloody surprise," he insisted and then exhaled a long, exaggerated breath. "No, I've loved one. She happened a long time ago, an innocent different kind of love. The love of an idealistic and naive man."

"I'm sorry."

"You don't have to be. The love I shared with Carrin is not the same love I share with you. Love is rare in my line of work."

A pinch of a challenge pricked Holly, and she decided to change the subject since it appeared Luka had finished sharing about Carrin.

"Can I ask about the sensational rumors surrounding sex in the rock music world? After what I witnessed backstage at the *Bon Jour* concert, I wonder, how many women would you say you've engaged in various types of sexual act with over the years? Fifty? Seventy-five?"

Luka's face spread with a surprised look at her question, then settled into a sense of wonderment.

"Miss Hill, is this an interview? Or, are you wondering where you fall on my list of conquest before I found you?" His answer came as more of a challenge. "Would you believe me if I said you're at the end of the list? That no more will follow you."

"Let's say, I do want an approximation of how many it took to find me?"

Luka seemed to like her sparring with him but settled into a pensive look. His eyebrows met seriously in the center of his wrinkled forehead. "I've never thought to count them, Babe. Let's say as a lad I took full advantage of the situation."

Holly fired again, "A hundred?"

Luka's face didn't acknowledge the numbers.

"More?"

And he shook his head yes.

"Hundred and fifty?"

And he shook his head again.

"More?"

"Yes. What's the bloody difference? I've found you. You're here." He kissed her neck, reminding her of his proximity.

"How many?" She pushed, almost demanding.

"I'm not certain." He maintained, clearly impatient for the questioning to end.

"Somewhere around four figures. Might be more, I suppose. Life was different. I can remember Kaine, and I use to throw parties at Briarwood Cottage and try to pick out the virgins and take them out back to the boathouse to have a go. I think he holds the record for seven in one night."

"You're kidding? Kaine! You make it sound cold and predatory. Tell me that happened as a one–time game?"

"For young chaps climbing to the top, it became a great sport in those days. Remember, we weren't faced with a social disease that killed. The truth is, we were a lot of randy lads all the time, and we seized the opportunities that became part of our life and being bad chaps. The groupies expected us to fuck them, and they wanted to suck us. These days those stories sound like an excuse. But back then...."

Holly sat astonished. "Tell me about the old days."

Luka pulled Holly into his arms, hugged her quickly, and started to fade into the past and his memories.

"Different world, entirely bloody different."

Then he leaned back and sipped on a cuppa tea.

Holly watched him vanish into the past, and when he started to tell his story, she sat flabbergasted.

"At twelve, I snuck out with my mates at boarding school to see John Roberts play his last gig with his first band in London. I didn't appreciate it then, but it's turned out to be the finest concert I've ever attended and turned out to be a turning point. I walked out that night knowing I wanted to play guitar. I attended the equivalent of what Americans would call an ivy–league private school called Eton." His voice started to trail into memories.

"Eton? Of course, I'm aware of that school. It is posh, the best are accepted. Oh, Luka, you do surprise me at every turn."

"Do I?"

"Yes. Sometimes you're like a chameleon, others you stand out as brilliantly as the sun."

Luka bent down and kissed the top of her hair affectionately.

"You do say the most curious things, Babe."

He shrugged his shoulders and took another sip of tea.

"Eventually, the invitation arrived, and I was sent down, oh, you'd call it expelled, because I ignored my studies by sneaking out to the pubs. Apparently, my attitude challenged the headmaster. He made my life bloody hell, making it clear I would never amount to anything if I continued on that road I'd be sent down.

"My father heartily agreed — the bastard. But being wealthy and well connected, he arranged to have me placed in a special school with a stronger reputation for handling difficult and spoiled chaps like me. I did a runner again and again. Even me mum, who lived in France, sided with my father, and since, we've never been close. Fuck them, I thought. They agreed, and I told my father to sod off.

"I bummed around England, and by seventeen, I'd been in a few bands. And then I met Jaden, and we played in a band together for a while, about six months, a smashing good time, probably best of my life."

Holly leaned back to note his satisfied grin, showing her his joy remembering his good times. She moved closer and kissed his warm cheek.

"Go on Angel Eyes."

"Like all bands, the personnel changed. I wandered around for a while, drifting into touring bands, seeing a little of Europe and recorded a pair of demo records. But I never liked the way they treated me as a musician assuming me to be stupid and of lower class. Eventually, I wanted to do more with the money end. To show those buggers, that even with long hair, I would out think them. I decided to form my own band. I eventually hit in England."

"You're a rock star?"

"For a while, but I'd say more of a Pop Star. A string of number one singles followed, and I acquired a bit of European attention. I appeared in magazines and on local telly shows. I built enough of a following and recognition to start considering the American market."

Luka threw his head back, allowing his hair to slide down his back. This seemed to be a crossroads of a sort in his story. His face tensed, the joy instantly drained from his sparkling eyes.

"Anyway, Sarah."

"Sarah?" Holly interrupted. "That bitch knew you first?"

"Remember, I told you in London, I've known Sarah Cromwell all my life. Her father's the caretaker for Sinclare

Estate. That's my family's estate next to Briarwood Estate. I grew up with Emily Dunnehill, or, as she known, as Emily Jamison, sister to your once intended."

"Your last name is Sinclare?" She had it!

"Yeah. Not something I care to publicize."

The sting in her chest told her to keep her mouth shut to keep Luka talking.

"I would have most likely met Kaine earlier if I hadn't been on the road touring when he arrived from America. But I digress. Sarah met Kaine and instantly became obsessed with him, a pattern that would follow him with all women he met. She brought him 'round to one of my shows to show off her new chap.

"A few months later, she'd heard a rumor I'd changed musicians in the band and wanted me to consider Kaine. He played rhythm guitar and as a package, I could hire, Ian on the keyboard.

"But Kaine possessed an unforgettable voice. I followed my strong premonition that fateful day and I eventually hired the pair of them. I continued as front man and lead guitarist. The girls loved us. And we could make it, because, besides the talent, we were an unusually pretty band if I do say so myself."

He laughed one of his joyous Luka laughs, filling the whole room.

Holly joined in deliriously happy Luka finally shared his past with her. He didn't come across as arrogant or self-consumed with himself, but clear, he's always been aware of his effect on women.

"What happened?"

Holly asked excitedly, hoping to get close to the core

backstory of *Hurrikaine's* rise to fame and glory that she'd failed to turn up from her extensive research. She continued to feed Luka small slices of apple encouraging him to unravel his story.

"My being a few years older and more experienced than either of them helped, but Kaine wrote and sang, and performed country songs in bars. We toured with a few hit singles and on our way until I developed fucking polyps on my throat, which eventually required surgery. Back then, we didn't have the high technology as in England. I underwent the necessary surgery, but something went wrong. I've never been able to sing with the intensity, durability or clarity I'd had before, so Kaine took over for me. And it hurt, Babe. I couldn't sing anymore. I loved singing more than anything else in the world."

Holly slid closer to Luka wishing her kisses to be an elixir to wipe away the storm of sadness rising in his eyes. She ran her fingers through his hair as a gesture of comfort and listened.

"It was only a matter of time, and the girls swarmed all over him. He became the front man."

Holly listened to the familiar story.

"You've read the story, Babe. You should have found the press version in your research."

"Yes, I did. But it never said anything about you."

"I used the luxury of re-creating history and omitting this section from the *Hurrikaine* legend."

What an understatement. She'd read the watered down version of the great advent of *Hurrikaine*. But never a word that the band had been created out of Luka's suffering.

"Luka, please, you tell me the real story."

"The real story...." He took a deep breath and slowly exhaled. "I've changed the story often. I forget the definitive version."

"Tell me what you can."

"At my insistence, we changed the name of the band, spelling from *Hurricane*, *Hurri-K-A-I-N-E*, to match the spelling of the new lead singer's name. That did it. Everyone took to him. The band recorded a ballad I wrote with Kaine as the vocalist. At the time, my anger ran out of control from what life dealt me. I wouldn't let them release it. After a bit of commercial success, they finally convinced me to release it, *One Love*. As you read, it went multi-platinum globally without me on it. Without me fucking on it, Babe!

"Back to the beginning. The offers streamed in steadily, and I didn't like the asshole managing us. When the contract ran out, I took over their management. They needed me, and me, them. I threw myself into the business of taking care of the band, but my throat hadn't healed. At that point, Kaine replaced me. The rejection nearly finished me. I quit playing guitar and became the band's manager and later their producer."

Holly cautiously proceeded to ask the question he carefully managed to avoid answering. "I don't understand the reason for the competition between you and Kaine? With all the research I've done on *Hurrikaine*, it's clear to me and to the world, without you, Kaine would never have become the megastar he is."

Luka turned a bit to allow the moon's silvery beam to shadow his perfectly sculptured face. His eyes once filled with lust, looked at her laced with heavy pain, more pain than she'd ever suspected Luka of hiding. And then he'd called her by her name.

"Holly, I've never told anyone this, but it would seem that I'm comfortable with you. And in a way, I haven't been in many years. Not since...."

He looked to her, and she saw the redness lying in wait in his eyes, telling her, he fought to hold back his tears.

She kissed his soft furry cheek. "Are you thinking of Carrin?"

Luka didn't move or acknowledge the name spoken. The bluesy music became known, piercing the shroud between them. She pushed the moments to the back of her mind. She needed the rest of the story. And how long it would be before he ever chose to speak up again?

"It would seem I have confessed many of my secrets to you. The truth has been extremely difficult for me to accept after all these years." Luka turned to look at her as if struggling to find the right words. "I worked on the road playing and singing for years. I never went as far as Kaine did in the same amount of time.

"And Kaine?

"Nothing would stop Kaine from what he has become. I didn't see it straightaway, but soon it became apparent that he would be a mega superstar.

"I held on, preparing for the inevitable. I'm aware I have a reputation for taking Kaine to the top.

"But seriously? How does one bloody harness a comet fated to become the most successful singer of his time?"

Luka's chin drooped, the tips of his long hair floated on the top of the cool water.

Holly placed her hand at the base of his neck and started to massage his tight and taunt muscles. Her strong intuition knew there'd been more to the story.

She moved closer. She pulled back a long lock of his hair and hung it over his ear. She leaned in and left a trail of kisses along his neck up to the line of his chin and she paused to acknowledge.

"You're extremely successful.

"You've become what most boys growing up want to be.

"You dreamed of becoming honored and respected in your field — you're revered.

"You're stinking, filthy rich and without your father's influence.

"You have all the power need.

"You own stock in CMT.

"You're always confident and hopelessly sexy.

"You have everything Kaine has if not more. What is it between you two?"

Luka turned his head while he raised his chest to catch another ragged breath, a deep, soulful breath as if rounding up all his courage.

Holly braced herself for his answer. She saw the fire in his eyes — no, more intense than fire.

Maybe jealousy — maybe fear of Kaine.

The light grew brighter, fiercer, and she observed the hate flow freely as Luka started to speak.

Chapter Nineteen

KILLER IN ME

L uka Hunter finally needed her.

Holly looked down to see how he held her hand. He gripped it tightly, and she'd never let him see it hurt.

"I remember the rumors in the newspapers when Kaine arrived from America after his mother's death. Kaine Walker, the prodigal son of Duke Edward Dunnehill, the third — life friend of my father's and next-door neighbor. What is difficult for American's to understand is how ingrained appearance and title is in English society. Everything is exaggerated with personal loyalties constantly on public display, and then mixed with a royal peerage, it can be tricky. Add to it family expectations and duty to country, everything becomes overblown and important to all involved.

"My father held a title, Lord Sinclare, due to his nominated, and appointment by the Queen when he took a seat in the House of Lords. And not to bore you with England executive branches, but The House of Lords is the upper chamber of the two houses of Parliament, and the title cannot be passed on to future generations. My father never allowed anyone to forget that, especially when he would rage on his alcoholic binges. I fell into competition for my father's attention with the alcohol, but I worried because I could never give him the one thing he valued most — my own English title.

"It became necessary I become as important as any man with a title in England. I'd fantasize he would stop drinking, show me attention, and be proud of me. But that became impossible. Without rank and title, I'm merely another wealthy Englishman. And Lord Alexander Maxwell Sinclare, my father, never let me forget it either. Since I'm not of bloodline, what I am is known as a commoner, never able to become royalty with no road available to gain title as my father unless nominated and the palace appointed me, deeming my accomplishments as worthy. My father died a few years ago believing me to be a failure in his eyes.

"I want a drink," Luka grumbled under his breath.

"That won't change anything except damage you more."

Holly put her arms around Luka to hold him close, to comfort him. But he'd said it again, his sir name — Sinclare. Confused by all the English title business or peerage as they called it she asked.

"What does all this English title have to do with you and Kaine?"

"It is ancient history. Everyone in the world knows Kaine's story except you Babe. How he inherited his royal title after the death of his father. And I have suspicions, there's more to Edward Dunnehill's death than what has been made public. I'm convinced the palace covered up Edward's real cause of death I feel it in my gut. But I've no proof except the ravings of a drunk, my father." Luka stopped and took a breath.

And Holly wondered if she should encourage him to tell more?

But Luka started to speak again. And her future hung on every word he shared.

"Kaine inherited the title the new Duke of Dunnehill. But what secretly devastated me, given my history with my father, the fucker threw it all away. His title.

"All I ever wanted as a lad. I'd be bloody well pressed to find an Englishman, who deep down inside, didn't want the title. How could I complain? As an only child, I would inherit great wealth and all the privileges that come with money. In spite of my father's raging addiction to drink as he drifted into middle age he enjoyed his title and all that came with it. But I would never become royalty. And here comes Kaine, Duke of Briarwood. But the twist? He's raised with American values.

"After Kaine found out his title meant no abdication, he simply turned his back on title and duty. I'm not stupid. I milked it. At that time in history, England faced tough economic and social times. The great anger and outrage toward Parliament, the new woman Prime Minister, and the palace meant fertile soil for *Hurrikaine*. I planted stories in newspapers and magazines portraying Kaine as the bastard he truly was. The newspapers ate it for breakfast and made Kaine the new anti-hero, and record sales broke all the established lines."

Holly cleared her throat, and holding his hand, thought to say.

"I seemed to remember something in the headlines and

a Royal Rocker. I don't understand how I've missed that in my research."

"Everyone remembers that. And after "One Love" became the band's first global hit, Kaine attracted all the birds, and the media followed him. His pockets were filled with money and the best drugs money could buy. The world became his and nothing was ever the same for me. I don't mean to sound like a pratt, but Holly ... this is what stings. He lived my life and ...""

Luka leaned in closer searching Holly's eyes for understanding.

She noticed how confessing became more and more difficult for Luka.

"...and I hated him. I did Holly. I hated him. Kaine inherited a fucking English title, my band, my song ... my place — my life."

Holly sat stunned. Luka held every right to his jealousy over Kaine. It would seem none of the people associated with *Hurrikaine,* realized how much he'd been broke by Kaine's usurping his position.

"Luka, I don't have the words to ease your pain, but I would have never guessed, you of all men would have ever wanted anything different from whom and what you are. I'm sorry, Luka."

Holly consoled him and then shook her hand free from his and slid her arm around his shoulders. The other snaked around his waist, and she hugged him tightly.

"Your secret is safe with me. You can trust me."

"I understand, Holly. I do."

And that brought a small smile to her face. Yes, the mighty Luka Hunter did trust her to see his weakness, his obsessive hatred of Kaine. He'd carried this pain of jealousy and envy for way too long and exploded, infecting him, clouding his mind, eating away at him. Perhaps with talking about it with her, he would start to heal.

Holly sat in the cool water, listening to the alto saxophone wailing hauntingly in the background. She gazed out the glass window lining the tub and was positive the stars in the heavens weeping.

After another soft, soulful song had finished, Luka flicked a piece of his hair back. He moved an inch or two. He slid his hand up to cup the back of her head.

Holly leaned her head back to rest in his strong hand.

He stared right into her eyes. His beautiful angel-eyes blinked to clear the rim of a thin pinkish veil.

"I have never sung "One Love" until tonight. I don't know what happened for them to suggest it. But I can swear that if you hadn't been there, it would have never happened. And downstairs when you suggested I try to sing again, well, I promised myself, I would never allow myself to be put in a position for defeat or rejection again, Holly. Can you possibly understand? To play music and not succeed a second time? I'm not strong enough to take that.

"For a long time, I dreamed of nothing but killing Kaine. My hatred for him grew, deep, and distorted. I blamed him ... I simply wanted him dead.

"Then I realized the climb to the top and his love of excess would kill him, and would serve him right. But the fucker's stronger than I once thought. That's when I realized he'd walk the path to greatness."

Holly took a long needed breath and sat back. Luka dropped his hand down around her lower back. She understood what everyone warned her about, the terrifying secret never spoke aloud until that moment. They all understood Luka's hatred eating away at him one day at a time. The included Kaine. She finally understood all their fears. They'd expected Luka to break. That he would one day lash out and kill Kaine. Ironically, Kaine became too important to Luka.

Kaine was not his enemy as Luka believed. Instead, Kaine became his muse in life, the goal ... the reason to be. To defeat Kaine would take the struggle and meaning away from his existence. Holly finally understood. Luka's hatred of Kaine fueled him. It gave him the necessary strength to beat the odds they faced together. Kaine once told her that. Luka figured Kaine would fail, but he always met the challenge. And those challenges made them into a billion dollar music machine.

Absolutely, amazing!

Then Holly recognized that Luka didn't need Kaine. No, Luka would never kill Kaine. She suspected he would never admit it.

On the other hand, wasn't it possible that Luka loved Kaine the most of all of them? Luka once warned her in London that Kaine would hurt the one closest to him. But that hadn't turned out to be her but Luka. He was closer to Kaine than anyone. After all, where would Kaine be without Luka to smooth the way and keep the legend of Kaine alive?

Luka admitted that Kaine went further in his career than Luka did in the same amount of time.

But Kaine had Luka.

Luka didn't have that advantage.

She'd finally ferreted out the motives — plain old

jealousy and hatred.

Why everyone thought, Luka could kill.

But now what?

Luka Hunter, amazingly complex. And yes, the situation remained volatile — anything was possible.

Kaine was coming.

Holly held onto Luka, his heartbeats thundered as if breaking into thousands of tiny pieces, threatening to pierce his flesh and bleed on her chest.

And not meaning to whisper while she stroked his head offered. "What an awful life you have spent with Kaine."

He nodded his head in agreement.

But she needed an explanation.

"Why did you stay?"

Luka closed his eyes, cocked his head to one side, and trying to muster his refined pride, turned his head toward the window. He opened his eyes and stared out into the clear night.

"I couldn't call it quits. I needed to fucking measure up next to him ... to soldier on as me Dad would say. I couldn't bloody well crawl off and hide. That's when I decided to change. I got clean and sober. I needed to prove I could beat him."

Holly stroked his long, damp hair kissing the side of his head. Had this man ever been loved? He seemed to crave her constant affection. And the ugly thought reared its defiant head forced to seek the answer, she hesitantly asked in a quiet, non-judgmental voice.

"Have you beat Kaine?"

Luka flicked his head back as if struck by a blow to his face. He turned slowly, scaring her. He stared straight into her eyes.

She wearily anticipated his reply.

"No, to beat someone, there has to be a winner and someone has to lose. To win there has to be a game. The problem with Kaine has been he's never playing a game. He simply is — he is real."

Holly sat holding on to Luka, stroking his hair. The terror of his confessions slowly incited horrid thoughts. How terrible. She understood that even if forced to remain with Luka she would never be free of Kaine. He's as much Luka's ghost as hers. Kaine's assessment was right in London. They always would be the Unholy Trinity.

Luka's admissions opened the doorway to her memories, which pressed relentlessly on her psyche. Kaine, expected in four days, and she realized she shamelessly counted the hours. Soon Kaine would be standing before her cloaked in an invincible confidence of a future together.

Holly sat reeling from Luka's startling confession of murderous desires, motivated by hatred. How should she handle this? She and her child caught in the crossfire of Kaine Walker the *Hurrikaine* and Luka. Or, Luka, was he's the hurricane? The destructible force that threatened all involved.

What an experience!

Both men electrifying, passionate and powerful, paired together by a quirk of fate, and as a result, their lives interlocked forever. And the more she thought about it, the more she came to believe she was the prize — the crowning glory. And that realization no longer flattered her. It was dangerous, could be deadly.

Everyone — right all along about Luka.

She's the checkmate.

Holly looked at Luka, seriously looked at him, too beautiful for words to describe. How could her lover with the angel-eyes be that malevolent? Even more mystified, she couldn't help but wonder how aware are Kaine and Luka of this delicate situation? Hell, she suspected Luka's always been on top of the situation as the master of manipulations.

Or, did he get things done?

Holly faced the facts that Luka and Kaine always seemed miles ahead of her.

Of course, Luka already anticipated Kaine's every move. That included Kaine's famed arrival in California, at the posh five-star hotel, The New Rochelle, in South Pasadena in a few days — the destination for Ian and Solange's wedding on New Year's Eve night. Would the crowning moment for Luka be when she walked in on his arm? The victory sweeter because Kaine would finally realize there was a game, to win her — and too late! Luka won her, the CMT stocks, and his child.

Luka, the winner!

He'd won it all.

NO ORDINARY LOVE

L uka never spoke a word. His arm dropped to her waist and held her balance as she stood beside him. Her eyes swept down the length of his flushed body from the bath, the way she loved him. His sexy grin met her eyes when they swept up to his face, the face of an angel.

She thought to take a breath, and she realized how much more she cared about him each time he opened up and shared his imprisoning past with her. And especially glad to learn that his jaded ideas about women never prevented him from showing her his intense passion and love for her.

Luka held out his hand, palm up, waiting for her. How polite and charming, like an English gentleman. She slipped her hand into his as she stepped into a large fluffy turquoise bath towel Luka held in his hands. He dried her body and then dropped the towel on the Spanish tiled floor. He kissed her as if to remind her whom she held in her arms and then picked her up and headed for the bed.

Luka crawled up her body to kiss her lips. He wrapped his arms behind her back and almost squeezed her lifeless. He jerked slight, aware of her sudden detachment. He tried to calm her by saying. "I've waited my whole life for you, Babe. I want to grow old with you, remember that. Promise me, no matter what happens."

"I can't promise."

She saw in his eyes how her choice of word affected him. Clearly, not what he expected, and not prepared to accept that answer.

There would be no gentleness. There would be no thoughts of tenderness. Luka entertained thoughts of Kaine in his mind as did Holly. The madness fired in their bodies. Luka needed to prove something.

And Holly accepted their fundamental bond – Kaine – a man that ignited their passion, a man who lived between them. As of these moments, they no longer hid from that truth. Kaine was coming for her. And Kaine would always haunt them.

No, untrue … because she would leave with him.

And what of Luka?

Holly ran her hands up and down Luka's hot body. His glorious hair covered her face like a web, and his hands worked her body roughly.

His kisses grew to become fierce and demanding. Luka slipped his tongue over her lips, dragging his moist lips down to her breast. His hot lips covered her cold skin and sucked as if in a rage.

The sharp pain reminded her of Kaine. Oh, how she remembered the roughness of Kaine. The message clear, he would never give her up to go to Kaine.

Luka raised himself over her. He'd sensed the moment, how she'd left him to think about Kaine.

And when her eyes met his, she saw it, the facts clear.

Luka would never willingly hand her over to Kaine ... as he'd said.

'Over my dead body.'

Luka moved swiftly, no longer stopping to pay homage to the child that dwelled inside her. His fingertips slid down her leg, kneading the inner side, softly at first, then more harshly and then mercilessly. He quickly pushed his hand along the path to its one destination. He took no time to separate the lips of her entrance to paradise, and with a fury. touched her where she loved his talent.

Soon her pleasure lost out to pain. Luka took out his pain and suffering on her, hurting her. His demons driving him and she endured the full extent of their power, as Luka mixed passion with flesh, pain with pleasure. His tricks not a new delight for her to enjoy.

Luka dropped, lost at the moment as he moved further down her body. Time for his chance to prove he alone could make her happy, he alone would love her. He replaced his fingers with his mouth. Passion exploded from Luka demanding her full attention as his skilled tongue sucked her opening bud, like touching lightning and propelled her to the magical place as her hands shot down to pull him closer.

Holly held on to his long, lush, golden hair, wrapping her fingers around it and held on to him, realizing she would never fully understand why Luka loved her. But before she could think a clear thought, the release started to build, on its way, promising to be harsh and furious. She pulled with all her might, wrapping her fingers around a lock of his hair, her own demons fighting each other. They screamed out from deep within her soul, louder, drowning out one after the other until all she could speak, one word — Luka.

Luka became a man with a cause. He wouldn't stop, and her body vacillated between exultation and anguish, knowing she would find no relief until Luka decided to finish. How long would Luka kiss her sweetness? Lick her moisture. But Luka showed no mercy, no awareness. He pulled hot, intense emotions from her and she didn't have their names.

The master unleashed his personal brand of exquisite passion. To describe him as a dedicated lover, too tame, one hell of a talented man, too condescending. But in those moments, he became Luka, unfettered, showing her how far into the madness of loving her he would go.

And the evil became a powerful aphrodisiac.

Luka broke away from her like a brilliant flash of lightning to slither up her wet, loved drenched body. Holly succumbed to Luka as he moved his body the length of hers, sliding on the sweat of their love. His face arrived first. His body second, his beautiful sex last. He'd paused for a moment, to stare deeply into her eyes. He hypnotized her, telling her to forget Kaine. This Luka moved with a single goal to make her forget.

Luka entered between breaths and filled her. The tip of him driving deep. He relaxed and arched his back, and once again, he moved inside her, deeply, purposely, setting the maddening rhythm she followed, again and again. The sounds of their passion broke free from their throats. He showed her how perfect her love matched his. He didn't need any tricks or impressive positions to drop her into his madness. His wish, to pleasure her, to make her forget, to love her.

Holly wanted to let go of her selfishness and give

herself to him, to this man with the angelic face, as he covered her with a curtain of his golden hair, her wish to match his, to pleasure him. That's when she realized she'd gotten it all backward.

She needed to make him forget ... to forget Kaine would take her away.

With the rhythm set, she moved to join him, digging her heels in, raising her body to take all of him, each luscious stroke. He raised himself onto his elbows, and then up as if ready to do a push-up, he pushed his hips higher, sending her head to hit the headboard. Pinned, the way he liked her. Each stroke fiercer than the last, hitting the top of her, ringing her bells every time.

Luka summoned his expertise, assuring her surrender.

Holly did all she could to hold on to him, to stay with him, but he was lost in her. And his lunges became as if each his last breath, drawing them out long and purposeful. Her sighs escaped, his name poured forth, and then the scream as Luka prescribed. And for the first time, he moaned aloud ... pleasure filled sounds.

Oh yes, Luka arrived at Oblivion inside her, and she wrapped her legs around him, holding him in as he thrust again, and again and again. She looked up into his eyes. They opened, watching her, dark and mysterious eyes, the blue replaced with smoky lust.

And she saw Luka.

She frantically threw her arms around the lower part of Luka's back, matching each of his gyrating motions that scorched her spirit with his heat, pouring his seed into her. But it didn't help. His seed ran dead in her womb. She carried another's child.

And he lunged again and again.

She knew.

As did Luka.

He'd lost her.

Luka could never fuck Kaine out of her — no matter how tender or how wicked.

The question. Who would pay the price?

"Luka," she screamed aloud.

Chapter Twenty-One

PROMISES IN THE DARK

Holly clung to Luka tightly as if those may be one of the last moments she'd ever be this close to him. She steadied her flailing body as Luka continued to thrust inside her almost as if out-of-control, almost as if he'd discovered a way to fuck Kaine out of her if he kept up the intensity. And Luka's agitated state served to exhaust him. Soon the warmth of his seed started to seep from her while he lunged again and again.

He'd read her mind, and was afraid, understanding she would never be this close to him again. With one last determined lunge, Luka froze inside her, pushing the last of the wind from her lungs.

Holly swallowed a gasp, as she sucked in the cool, fresh morning air.

Luka wrapped his body around hers, and he turned her head to see the golden sun announce another day with him. It rose majestically over the spiky peaks of the craggily shaped mountain range, splashing a vivid persimmon color against the black suffocating clouds creating a breathtaking backdrop. A sudden shudder ran up her back as she watched the dark clouds brooding, arriving to block out the sun, flashing an emergency warning, storm coming.

Kaine — in a matter of hours.

The anxiety continued building in all concerned.

Luka kissed Holly's cheek, drawing her lips to his. He called her to him, frantically doing his best to spread his magic and make her forget Kaine. He pulled on her bottom lip quietly sucking it between his with love and tenderness. He drew her to him as he slid off her body and then released her lips. He laid his head on her breasts as if listening and counting the beats of her heart. Then he rolled over onto his back and shut his eyes, his hair spread as a golden crown above his angelic face. He lay quietly on the crumpled bed sheet.

The cold air rushed in covering Holly's wet, steamy body. She looked at Luka with his hair stuck to his love-drenched face and damp shoulders. He drew in another refreshing breath, trying to enjoy the ride down from his mighty climax. But not with the usual peacefulness on his face. He opened his eyes, and they expressed it all.

Kaine was coming.

He lay quiet, for a long while as if planning his next move, knowing he'd already lost her to Kaine. But Luka always got what he wanted— but not this time.

He'd made a decision as if not satisfied with the way he'd loved her and whispered in her ear.

"Babe, there's a lot more I want to show you."

Luka took her arms and stretched them up while he sucked on her nipple, then stretched them out as if his prisoner to do with as he pleased as if he'd forgotten who he touched and she'd become another in a long list of women there to please him and his whims.

Luka's authoritative tone said she would comply as he rolled her on her side.

"Babe, I fancy this." His tone a strongly worded request.

"You will do this with me."

He moved.

"Relax. Enjoy the depth of the penetration." And he put on a condom.

Holly didn't understand his sharp insistence. She didn't want to comply.

However, he pushed, clearly persistent. "Try, Babe. Trust me. There are all kinds of pleasure, relax."

He closed the distance between them placing his body behind hers. At first, as he caressed her breasts and then flicked each nipple knowing this would add to her fire. And then he moved to follow the length of her body and bent her. He placed his magic finger near her back entrance and circled, relaxing her. At first, she found the act unnatural, not a necessary expression of love for her. But a new appetite of Luka's flared, and she found it uncomfortable, and she didn't want to participate. Within seconds, the prevailing evidence of his lust pressed against her derrière.

He promised, "I'll move slow, relax, enjoy." He moved, slow.

She cried out, the pain arrived.

He froze his lower body but continued stroking her breasts, kissing her neck.

"Okay, luv?"

Holly's breathing ran shallow, relieved she couldn't gaze into his eyes any longer. His chest moved, brushing against her back as his arm squeezed between her body and the bed and up until his elbow bent and his hand cupped the closest breast. His other hand closed over her upper arm to cup her other breast.

Holly lay on her side watching the black foreboding storm clouds approaching, the sun fighting to peek between them. She tried to relax, to open, to receive him while the thunder brought the uncertainty of doom, like Luka, determined to vent whatever demons that drove him. She laid there thankful Kaine didn't witness this by lurking in the shadows to see her screaming out again from the pain and terror of Luka's brutal act.

He moved.

She panicked realizing the full idea of his intentions, and she screamed out repeatedly.

"I can't ... I can't..."

Luka froze, hugging her.

"It's okay my beauty. Enough for 'now'."

It wasn't enough, for now, it would never happen again.

Either Luka's appetite was escalating, or his comfort level with her afforded him a safe place to reveal his true desires and allowed them to become known. What would she do? What would sex with Luka be like when she became his complete captive? What other unimaginable horrors awaited her?

She stopped him.

He'd listened because he lived in the throes of his strange love and wanted to please her. But what would happen when his focus centered on her satisfying him? What would she endure with Luka fully unrestrained? Used to having his every fantasy fulfilled. Yes, he'd scared her.

Luka Hunter was dropping his facade layer by layer. And all she could think … Kaine.

A few hours, all she needed to bare, and then never allow thoughts of this type of penetration ever again. Luka Hunter tried to fuck her to death by any and every way he held in his vast arsenal of sex techniques, and he certainly was prepared to unleash them all to kill the ghost of Kaine. With his arms wrapped around her protectively, Luka eventually drifted into a fitful sleep.

Holly lay for a long time planning her escape and then finally joined him in a restless sleep.

Kaine called to her from the doorway, but the light's glow was too dim to make out much more than his silhouette. Her heart fluttered, her dream lover returned. His cologne filled the room as he floated closer, his lips moving, saying something to her. Frustrated, she could barely hear his voice, and she reached out to pull him nearer.

Closer and closer, he came until he stepped out of the shadows into the light. Her Kaine stood handsomely as ever. He caused her heart to skip a beat, stealing her breath away. Kaine's dreamy voice spoke soft and languid, making it difficult to distinguish his words.

He drew closer, almost close enough to touch her, yet kept his distance.

She stretched her arms out to reach him, to touch him, to welcome him, to love him.

Kaine looked down at her laying on the bed. He lifted the turquoise sheet and slid in beside her.

His breath was warm and sweet.

His voice a mere whisper.

"I'm back."

Chapter Twenty-Two

TELL ME

Four Days — Kaine

Holly sat up with a start! The vivid dream too real. A private moment with Kaine in London came flooding back. She remembered when riding the motorcycle on their way to Briarwood Castle. How he'd stopped to sit under a tree and placed his head in her lap. How carefree and loving those moments were.

Kaine's intentions were to once again, climb into her bed to lie between her and Luka. He refused to be banished from her memories, struggling to remind her, he was coming for her.

"No." She wailed.

She startled Luka forcing him to rise beside her.

"What? What, Babe?"

Before she realized what she said, the words tumbled out.

"What am I going to do?" She asked in a panic, as her

hand rose to cover his cheek and traced his swollen, red lips from kissing her.

"He's coming." And she fell on his chest where he automatically pulled her into his loving arms, wrapped them around her securely to comfort her.

Luka squeezed her tighter, attempting to comfort her with words she doubted he believed himself.

"Kaine can't harm you anymore, Babe. I won't let him."

"But Luka, he's not coming to harm me. He's coming back for me because he loves me."

"No matter. Don't think any more about him. We have each other and a new life together. Go back to sleep, Babe. I'll hold you until you're dreaming sweet dreams of our life together."

Her body shivered.

Holly knew better.

Kaine was coming for her.

Holly tried to relax, slow to let her guard down with Luka. She closed her eyes and pictured Kaine's perfect body next to hers, warm and inviting. For a moment, she wondered who would be there if she opened her eyes, to see who lay next to her. She squeezed her eyes tightly closed, and her hand slipped up his body to his face and caressed the pricking of a day's growth of facial hair. She exhaled a sigh of relief. She opened her eyes a slit, to peek out, enough to confirm this lover as Luka.

Disoriented and confused by the darkness surrounding her, she peeked at the clock to see the time declaring it was early afternoon. She snuggled deeper into Luka's arms wondering if these would be her last moments with him like this. She forced opened her eyes and looked to Luka resting, laying on his back, his hair disheveled and fanned on the pillow. A peaceful look rested on his face, his chest breathing deeply. And she asked herself once again. Did she ever love Luka Hunter?

He moved nudging her, alerting her he too lay awake. He pulled her up to him, strong — so strong. And he arranged her body to support bent knees, ready to take the strength of him. He guided his unbreakable love inside her and drove her body down on his, shoving up as far as allowed.

She couldn't decide if she should surrender. What awaited her? Before she made a decision, he moved deeper to fit perfectly, and she arched her back to take more. She needed him. To hurt her again if necessary. To be able to tell which man she was fucking.

This man brought his talent, this man Luka — a perfect man, no, but he loved her.

"Love me Luka. Love me as you can."

Shivers rippled through her body, leaning into Luka's sex, and with one complete thrust, she sat taking all the majesty of him again. The pain of him shattered her. She couldn't take all of him, and she pushed herself down on him again, reminding herself this man is Luka, not Kaine.

Holly placed her hands on each side of Luka. She found the rhythm that worked the best for her, pumping him steadily and pleasurably. She dripped wet, she desired him, and he fucked her with precision. More, she wanted more — more.

Closing in, Luka joined her, sliding his hands up her sweaty back, to hold onto the top of her shoulders. He pulled her down to him, indulging her with a giant dose of his sex, pounding and pulsating inside her. As usual, he thrust himself inside her again, reminding her again and again which man filled her. Making love, yes, yes. No, fucking, she knew. Luka, yes, fucking, and she heard her quiet confession pour forth easily, comfortably.

"Luka."

"Louder!"

"Luka!"

"Say it louder!"

Holly screamed out, falling deep into the black hole of her pleasure with her lover's name on her lips.

Kaine's name in her heart.

Chapter Twenty-Three

YOU BELONG TO ME

Radiant flashes of lightning bolts streaked across the vast Tucson sky. They exploded, piercing the ominous black clouds. Moments later the powerful energy rumbled in the sky so loudly the window panes shook violently threatening to shatter.

Holly hated being at the mercy of the erupting storm. It would bring back devastating memories of Jon dying in the plane crash — Kaine loving her at the castle — and him leaving her at the manor.

How she hated storms.

The menacing desert sky appeared intimidating and threatening both at once — an apt description of the situation brewing. She moved in closer to burrow into Luka's warm arms with each unnerving series of lightning strikes.

His voice seemed calm and soothing as he whispered.

"You're quivering. It's all right. Babe, we'll be fine."

She understood his words meant to comfort her, but they didn't. Holly turned away from his warmth.

Luka rose from the bed, leaving her to wrap up in the

heated sheets and to watch him stroll into the bathroom.

She stole a moment to admire his perfect naked body because she wouldn't see it much longer. She couldn't help wondering what he would do when she crushed this private Luka.

The admission assaulted her conscience, and she couldn't think about that then. She trailed Luka into the bathroom as if he the Pied Piper. She focused her attention on the hot shower, and the steam that demanded her muscles relax because her body ached with pain.

She looked at him.

No words passed between them.

Kaine was coming.

Luka stepped in next to her. The warm pulsating water washed away their scent of passion and lust, but mostly the affection they shared for hours. Down it flowed into the vortex of water, draining into the abyss.

Out of nowhere, Luka desperately swept her into his arms, urgently kissing her ever softly, making promises.

"Remember, Babe, I do care for you. It's going to get rough the next few days. Especially anticipating Kaine and then seeing him will stir up powerful emotions for both of us.

"I want you to remember, you're not alone. And never forget, you belong to me. You have me to stand by you, and I will, especially when Kaine won't listen to reason. Believe me. I can take care of him. I can stop Kaine."

She'd no problem believing that. The problem — she didn't want Kaine stopped. This reminded her of a time when she and Kaine bonded together to fight the imminent arrival of Luka. And here she lay with Luka. It hadn't worked with Kaine, and it wouldn't work now.

None of Luka's comforting words could wipe away any of the massive knots tied in her stomach.

Kaine recognized Luka as a stormy and fiery adversary, yet it never stopped Luka. He'd won her to this point.

Was Luka wise enough to fear Kaine?

Was this Luka's fear speaking?

Could Luka guarantee Kaine would not win?

She wanted to run. She wanted to hide. She wanted to avoid the confrontation. To get the hell out. Her survival instincts raged on high alert, leaving two choices.

Fight or flight?

Flight sounded perfect!

"Can you get us out of here? Go for a drive in the desert. I need something to do." She pleaded to Luka.

"Smashing idea. I'm keen to check my messages, the fax, and the usual, return any urgent calls. Then we're out of here straightaway."

Holly hoped for no emergencies waiting for him as she chose a bright red sweater and stretched her legs into a pair of his light blue Levi's and rolled up the cuffs. Her thickening waistline resisted, too finicky to have anything restrictive around it, and both orifices of her most private body area throbbed, was sore and tender.

She slipped on brown rough out boots and picked up her new black, suede poncho. She threw it on the couch near the front door and then joined Luka in the den as she braided her hair. She noted him wearing a bright blue cowboy shirt, dark denim Levi's with vertical, frayed rips, and like her, rough out boots. A subtle mix of outlaw and rocker, the way she loved him best. The crotch of his pants bulged with his half aroused sex, the other way she loved him.

He'd answered his messages then announced.

"It's urgent I ring Tessa when we get back, and Michael has planned another shoot for HHW. We are to catch the band's plane at ten tonight at the private airstrip behind the airport. But instead of returning to L.A., we are heading for New Mexico. He's arranged for you to film more interviews with the band touring for future segments on the show. We have a few hours until our call time. When we get back, we'll pack. Oh, and Marty called, said he left our names out at Old Tucson. A pair of old mates of mine is shooting a western mini-series, *The Poker Player*. I liked to see the old west captured on celluloid. Does that sound inviting?"

New Mexico? The panic rose quickly. How long would they be there? She'd planned this to be their last day and night together. That tomorrow she would be home making excuses and waiting for Kaine — not with Luka in New Mexico, keeping his bed warm — again!

Holly quickly remembered to cover her disappointment. Wondering if she would be able to fool him much longer. Yes, his trusting her made it easy to pretend with him but lying dropped her into a pit of guilt. And the nasty word started creeping in again.

Betrayal.

Her betrayal when she left him again for Kaine.

"Babe, interested?" He said breaking into her thoughts.

"Sounds wonderful. Who are we seeing?" She didn't care. It would give her time to come up with another plan.

"Let me surprise you," he challenged, with a mischievous sparkle in his eyes as he held his Levi jacket lined with the curling puffs of lamb's wool.

"Yes, Mr. Hunter," she invited, forcing a smile. "By all means, please surprise me."

Luka drove the Jeep along muddy roads.

Holly filled her lungs with crisp, clean desert air. She sat in awe of the incredibly simplistic beauty of the barren desert landscape. She wondered if Luka gained more confidence with the immediate threat of Kaine ten thousand miles away.

They arrived at a stop sign and then followed the directions to Old Tucson, leaving the imposing black storm far in the distance behind them. Holly discovered Old Tucson to be a famous television and movie location site and amazingly authentic re-creation of frontier life. She held on to Luka's hand, slowly strolling along the muddy streets heading for the sound stage, passing mock saloons, facades of merchant stores and the museum. They stopped along the route to appraise the exhibits. The sets were so real she almost heard the ghosts of another lifetime whispering to her, inviting her to come and pretend.

"It's as if our world doesn't exist," she informed him taking his hand to start her sojourn into the eighteen-nineties. Marty arrived and escorted them to the catered shoot. After introductions to the crewmembers, they stood eating a late lunch.

Luka leaned on a wooden beam outside the mock saloon. Luka looked appeared as if he lived there and fit in as natural as a wood barrel, and once again, clearing away any doubt what a handsome man he was, certainly movie star material. With a couple days' growth of beard to add to his attractiveness, she momentarily wished Outlaw Luka would capture her, use her, taking her where ever his lusty desires wanted — but in the next moment, she ended that fantasy. No, she was certain, she couldn't keep up the pretense of wanting him again.

Luka looked at her as if sensing the change. He stepped back to lean on the wall of the old saloon and brought her with him slipping his arms around her.

Holly melted into the curves of Luka's body, a perfect fit, always a perfect fit.

She spoke softly. "I can't take much more."

Luka's hand came up to cup her chin, and he held her lips a breath away from his.

"It's okay honey. It's the lightning in the distance and the storm spooking you." And then he kissed her longingly.

"You're safe." And then he kissed her again and squeezed her tight against him. He never seemed to get enough of her due to the other storm brewing. A storm in which she didn't wish to be caught.

Holly and Luka held each other as they stood near the train station, watching the next shot locked in each other's arms. To her surprise, two famous country singers waved them over in their direction.

Holly started to smile, then laughed aloud and looked up to Luka.

He kissed her lips quickly.

She spoke above a whisper, "Let me guess? Your old mates?"

He lifted one eyebrow and grinned sheepishly.

"Could be?"

Luka Hunter, a darling man, a delicious blend of coy and boyish one moment, but deadly and dangerous the next.

The actor/singers crossed over to Luka after the scene and after introductions to Holly, they caught up quickly, especially how Luka worked at CMT. And then the cantina jam came up and how they hadn't realized he sang either. And the singers talked about Luka joining them on an album.

Holly's head started to disengage from the chatter noticing the storm closing in fast.

The crew appeared anxious to get this last tedious shot in the can. Time to move and they held hands walking along the muddy streets locked deeply in their separate thoughts, seizing an occasional kiss, neither seeming to care, especially Luka. He was a man in love, and he no longer cared who saw it.

Cold wind blew red spots on their cheeks, and Luka kissed her and then suggested.

"Let's say goodbye. I want you in the worse way."

What could she say? She'd have to spend another night with him, and no way to stop him.

As the first wave of the storm started to tease those beneath with a powerful blast of rain, the Jeep started, and Luka spun out of the safety of the 1890's. They bravely drove west into the eye of the storm, and it gained on them fast. Luka barely pulled in the parkway of their desert estate before the heavy blankets of rain pounded loudly on the roof of the mansion. Coupled with the fierce desert wind, she stood at the window, watching the violent and destructive force of the battering rain smothering the submissive desert terrain. The dioramic scene momentarily frightened her and then she saw Kaine in her mind's eye.

Oh, my Precious One what are you going to do when

you see me.

Luka moved closer to fill in the lines of her body. "I have to ring Tessa, why don't you wait for me in bed?"

"Delicious thought!" She'd responded, seeing no way out. She continued to perfect her part as a compliant concubine.

"I hoped you'd say that." He turned her in his arms and gave her a sample of what awaited her.

After she let go of him, he headed for the den, his long hair blowing in the breeze of his gait. Instead of scurrying upstairs to primp and wait for Luka, she thought she should check the fax machine for any word from Lucy. As she approached the room beside the den, she listened to Luka raise his voice in an angry tone. Her first instinct, as usual, was to leave him alone, but instead, she wondered what transpired to make him angry? She shouldn't, but she couldn't stop herself from stopping to listen.

"No! I bloody well mean as soon as possible. I'm starting divorce proceedings the minute I return to California. I will marry Holly, the day it's legally possible."

Holly leaned back against the wall unfettered by his strong declaration of commitment to her. And to Tessa! She remembered the financial loss he'd told her he would suffer if she married him and everything and everyone around him became part of the Luka Hunter Production.

In fact, she noted, he'd started proceedings to file for divorce with a few false starts; apparently, they hadn't suited his production schedule.

"You heard me right. No! Never! The entire Asset collection ... the Asset line is mine. Without me and my connections, and let's not mention money, you wouldn't be what you are."

That did surprise Holly, not his finger in another enterprise, but the fact he wanted Asset. What did he want with a designer clothing line? It belonged to Tessa's and didn't Luka have enough money to last him a number of lifetimes? Wouldn't it smooth the waters of the settlement if he gave Tessa Asset outright?

And it hit her rumbling through her like a night terror.

He owned her show.

This would be how he'd treat her when she started to break away from him. With all his power and money, she'd have no way to fight him, escape him.

"Tess, your bloody threats don't scare me."

He paused.

Then Holly heard.

"That's bollocks. You'll never kill me, Baby."

The sarcasm lay thick, and Luka's usually calm voice became quickly irritated again.

Holly tensed as she listened.

He laughed again, "... over my dead body. That's what it will bloody well take! I'd rather see your whole bleeding clothing line go up in flames first, then turn it over to you," he said with a heavy tone of maliciousness.

Shocked by the venomous sting in his disclosure, she had her answer if she'd tried to leave him.

"To hell with the insurance, dead people can't rebuild." he'd scoffed.

A frightening chill reverberated through Holly. He'd kill her if she left him. She debated if she should tip him off that she stood there. But with his guard down, she needed to know his intentions at this point.

"No. I don't bloody want you to buy me out, you cow. It's my stock. Asset is mine, Tessa. Understand? You can scream all you want, and the designs may damn well be in your pretty head, but I'm capable of making sure you never have a chance to remember anything, ever again."

His admission flattened Holly against the outer wall to remained out of his sight line. Finally, she'd heard for herself what everyone warned her about him. This conversation wasn't idle business vibrato. He'd seriously threatened Tessa's life. And it sounded similar to the threat Luka made in the canyon about Kaine.

Have something happen to him worse than rehab.

Finally, the shocking side of Luka, the ruthless businessman that made things happen that everyone alluded to and why they warned her to move cautiously. A side of Luka, she'd brushed up against, and her intuition told her to proceed with great caution. She'd known of his deviousness before she'd decided to board the jet, but she also realized it was not a smart move to alienate Luka Hunter. Believing she'd be safer next to him because as she'd learned quickly, he was dangerous, not her loving protector.

Luka's voice started to rise again.

"No, not a threat Tess. A promise. And I keep my promises."

He quieted as if listening, then laughed a wicked, sinister laugh.

"Such language, it doesn't become you, Baby. I'm ringing off straightaway, but not before giving you, a taste of what divorce will be like for you. Look for the petition the first of the year."

Then he quieted for a moment.

"Oh, yeah, fuck you too, you tart!"

Silence.

Holly heard what she guessed to be the cordless phone hit the brick fireplace, shattering with a loud crash. Holly quickly slipped away. She rapidly calculated that there would be three more days, and then Kaine would arrive, and he would handle Luka Hunter.

She made noise in the hallway to give him time to regain his composure, and then she would act as if she never overheard.

Holly entered the den, apprehension her closest companion, afraid of what she'd find. She watched him force a smile.

She queried, "Are we eating here or out?" She hoped to cover her nervousness.

Luka stood composed. The mask on his face gave none of his true thoughts away.

"Why don't we pack? We can eat on the plane."

He beamed with the usual sparkle in his eyes as if he returned from a conversation with Mary Poppins, not fresh from threatening his estranged wife's personal safety and security.

Say it, Holly, she thought, *he's threatened to murder Tessa if she attempted to obstruct his goal. The same fate that awaits you if you followed in Tessa's footsteps.*

The alarm went off in her head. If Luka masked his intense feelings that quickly, and that well, it would make him a master of disguises. Was any of what he'd told her the truth?

Luka walked up close to her, oh so close.

She looked up into his blue, beautiful eyes, eyes of an angel and she thought terrifying thoughts.

This man might physically injure her.

This man is in a powerful position to destroy her career.

But most importantly — if this man is truly twisted and in a strange love with her — when she left him to go back to Kaine — this man could kill her.

Chapter Twenty-Four

MILES AWAY (THE TRUTH IS)

Everything Holly once believed unraveled fast. The ink-stained clouds stretched out like octopus tentacles across the vast night sky, threatening to surround Holly's plane at the airport and hold her a captive. She held her every fear of flying in check, knowing tonight was a perfect night for a plane crash.

She wearily boarded the private touring jet and because her bottom ached, carefully plopped down into a vacant seat next to the guitar player. She guessed her face color as ashen, her knuckles twisted white from her grip on the arm of the seat. The plane took off smoothly with all her fears stamped clearly on her face.

Certain the hour's flight would unnerve her even further with the expected turbulence from the storm as predicted, it rocked the plane, reminding her of how quick a strong and fierce storm could take her down, down any moment, plummeting to the earth, to her death. But as close to a panic in recent memory she was, she was more afraid of Luka when he found out that she'd leave with Kaine.

The jet landed roughly, bouncing onto the icy tarmac

and then skidded to a dramatic halt in Albuquerque, New Mexico. The stop chilled her to the bone and surely represented another premonition that her life was in danger.

Bon Jour performed a concert that night at Tingley Coliseum. As expected, Luka already prepared Holly for meetings with the New Mexico affiliates and interviews with the remaining members of the band.

Three Days — Kaine

She traveled with Luka and the band in a comfortable minivan to the four-star hotel and was well into the early morning when she and Luka collapsed into each other's arms. Luka hungered for her, but Kaine seized her mind — Kaine — on his way to set her free from Luka.

"Babe, come to me. Kiss me. Touch me. Look at me with those eyes that say all they want is me."

Luka fumbled, having trouble getting her undressed, his words attempting to arouse her passions didn't work, and the awkward moment growing more difficult than she'd ever imagined. She attempted to concentrate on his exciting body. But nothing erased the images of Kaine's face constantly reappearing in her mind.

Finally, Luka leaned over and kissed her cheek, holding his emotions in tack and conceded as he squirmed uncomfortably.

"I'm already losing you aren't I, Babe?" He conceded as he squirmed uncomfortably.

Holly wanted to cry. She looked into his blue eyes-to-die-for, as his stinging words condemn her — his words announcing the truth.

She'd strayed, her heart running toward the eye of the *Hurrikaine*. Her silence became her answer, confirming his suspicion.

Luka did everything possible after he undressed her. His tricks, his positions, his passion tried to open her heart, tried to love her, hoping to convince her to return to him if merely in body. She gave him her tiny sighs and occasion moans of pleasure and then cries from pain, but she didn't speak his name.

The sun crept up barely lighting the dismal, black clouds that covered the Albuquerque sky. Holly slept fitfully, occasionally waking cradled in Luka's insecure arms. His warm hands cupped her breasts, and she listened to his heart beating rhythmically, his breaths caressing her ear. Their wake up call for noon came too soon, and tired, she stared through a crack in the drapes where snow magically and silently fell.

Luka started to stir, and the flesh and blood of him stood instantly aroused.

Holly estimated twenty-four hours were left then she'd be home safe in the canyon, free of Luka. She needed to pretend a bit longer.

And a pinch of guilt assaulted her.

She made love to his body with her thoughts of betrayal, picturing Kaine's face, his body until he spilled his seed.

She showered with him and dressed quickly to start her demanding afternoon of meetings and interviews. No matter how busy, or, how close Luka stood to her, all she thought, he's on his way — Kaine.

After strolling two hours with the band in the glistening fresh snow, shooting the final segment of her interview, she sat cold, soaked, and hungry.

Luka wrapped her in thermal blankets, then stuffed her in the heated van. He whisked her back to the hotel where she convinced him she needed to rest awhile then dressed to make the concert.

However, no matter where they went or what they did, the three of them traveled together. She and Luka, no longer alone — and they both knew it.

The second concert turned out to be more exciting for Holly after having the personal contact with the band. It made the experience much fuller though they avoided the backstage area and the women. Too many women, and on a two hundred stop tour all around the world that would mean more and more women. She understood why Luka said he'd been with thousands, as with Kaine.

Holly thought about London and *Hurrikaine*. Back to when Kaine invited her to travel with him to the high cities of Europe.

Holly lamented, sorry she'd missed the Super Star jet with Kaine, destination Paris.

This latest admission concerned her, understanding her fear of Luka's power.

Her new plan — the moment she saw Kaine, she would throw herself into his conquering arms, and beg for his forgiveness and quickly get as far away from Luka and Sarah as possible.

Holly's straying thoughts gave her away at the party after the concert, her situation taking its toll on her. She realized her growing fears certainly were etched upon her face.

And when she looked into the mirror in the lounge, she found a pale, drawn, exhausted face. Her weary brown eyes said it all.

Kaine, three days, and counting.

Chapter Twenty-Five

(FLESH AND BLOOD)
SACRIFICE

The impending situation became impossible for Holly. With no way to deny her strong feelings of doubt and confusion due to Kaine's imminent arrival, she worried constantly agitating her already heightened state of awareness. It wasn't that she didn't look forward to seeing him, she would see him *'ready or not, here I come'* as the old childhood rhyme went.

The longer she studied Luka's beautiful eyes, with each hour passing, the more they grew concerned. No longer did she find the sparkle she'd grown accustomed to — it vanished, replaced with growing anxiety. His fears of losing her made her more afraid too — of his reaction when he did.

Her luck turned when Luka brought over an invitation from a beautiful black woman and a welcomed reprieve.

"Look who I've run into, luv. This is Trina Lewis. We go back. I haven't seen her since she sold her screenplay a few years ago. You may have seen the blockbuster movie *Red Skies*. She's been hiding up in her cabin in the Sandia

Mountains, where she's working on her sequel and has invited us to stay overnight in her sanctuary. It will be more comfortable than the hotel, and I hoped to take your mind off things."

Holly looked at Luka, embarrassed by how she'd been behaving and told him with her eyes her sorrow for her actions.

Luka sheepishly grinned and then consoled. "We have to put everything out of our minds and enjoy our last night together."

Holly, taken aback by his comment delivered a surprised expression to her face. She blurted out. "Last night?"

"Sorry, lousy choice of words." He quickly corrected.

"I meant last night on this junket."

He feels it too!

She didn't need another reminder to have it all driven home, how much she looked forward to Kaine's return. Perhaps Luka meant the observation to test her, to see where her loyalties lay. Well, she'd passed with flying colors because Luka smiled. The dark cloud that laced his eyes lifted for the moment.

Trina was delightful, in her early thirties with short, black cropped hair, big beautiful black pools of luminous eyes. Trim, she dressed in a baggy sweater and leggings swirling with bright, bold colors. Her whole vibe expressed light and spirituality. Exactly what Holly needed to lift her spirits and persevere through the final hours until Kaine.

"Trina. Thank you, for inviting us. We're grateful for the seclusion."

Trina lit up with a bright, cheerful smile.

"Great. I'll pull the van around front in about a half hour. That should give you time to pack."

Luka leaned over and pecked Trina lightly on the cheek and Holly heard him add.

"I owe you one Trina, we need this."

Holly followed Luka over to the band, said their goodbyes, explaining how they would take a commercial jet home. They packed and left with Trina in her new beige van.

Trina drove up the winding mountain road to her home in the Sandia Mountains, entertaining them with her amusing antidotes as a writer trying to break through the race and gender barriers in Hollywood. They'd barely beat the foreboding snowstorm when they arrived at Trina's three-bedroom dream cabin.

Soon they sipped hot, herbal tea produced by the Apaches, a local indigenous tribe.

Trine fascinated Holly with her studied with an Apache medicine man for research on her film and inadvertently become a practicing medicine woman. Her cabin was chocked-full with amazing native artifacts. Her walls lined with jars filled with herbs and miles of bookcases stuffed with informative volumes.

Soon the room smelled pungent, and Trina explained she'd lit a mixture of sweetgrass with sage to bless their time together. Holly noticed a plethora of plants drying about the room, especially by the blazing hearth.

A large piece of redwood held candles for what Trina explained were the four directions. Holly asked about a pouch about her neck, and Trina described its significance.

"It's my medicine bag. It carries important pieces of my

experiences that represented my personal power."

But most important to Trina were the eagle feathers over her fireplace displayed in a case. She pointed out how illegal they were to own, but that she'd found them on the ground and took custodial care of them.

Holly instantly loved the cabin and the one bedroom converted into a state of the art office, sporting a spectacular mountain view. Trina sat at her new desktop computer where she'd mastered her craft of storytelling. Luka familiar with computers spoke of upgrading at CMT the first of the year.

Holly sighed. She'd been lucky because Lucy did all the word-processing on the computer, but eventually, she would have another complicated machine to learn.

Trina continued spinning yarns and told of legends about the local natives, keeping them up late sipping hot chocolate in front of the roaring fireplace.

Eventually, Trina invited them. "You both seem interested in Indian medicine and rituals, I can take you to a private and sacred hot springs in the morning, and perform a blessing ceremony."

Holly and Luka enthusiastically agreed to the adventure. They decided to turn in at that point and get a good night's sleep. Trina went on ahead, but as Holly passed the window, she looked out onto the freshly fallen snow and admired how the silvery moon, peeked through a crack in the white clouds. The silver rays shone down glistening on a pond of crystallized water.

"It is breathtaking up here Trina," Holly announced and then sighed.

"I wouldn't leave it for all the money in Hollywood,"

Trina responded as she stepped into her bedroom at the other end of the hall.

Holly understood what she meant. Like the desert, here the peace and the solitude refreshed and revitalized both the mind and body. And peace was what she desperately needed. Luka came up from behind her, slipped his arm around her waist, and leaned over to kiss her neck. She stopped him, turned to face him, and looked at his sad, apprehensive eyes and his words moved her to tears.

"I can see you pulling away, and it aches so bloody much because I don't know how to keep you with me. I'm afraid for the second time in my life, and I don't like it. And it's not Kaine I'm afraid of anymore. It's you. Of losing what we have, our future and that if anything, or anyone, comes between us, I'm not convinced what I would do?"

The words frightened her as he'd intended, but they also made him vulnerable. Luka showed her his pain, something he constantly guarded. No one could see his weaknesses. That she was a weakness in him and that upset him. She searched his eyes. The sparkle vanished, replaced with neediness and hoped for her reassurance, but she couldn't.

"Luka, I'm anxious too! Kaine's coming, and it has been a long time since I last saw him. My problem is remembering all the horrible circumstances that were created to rip us apart in the first place."

"You mean me. How I came between you and him at Friar Manor?"

"Partly, and I'm sorry you feel responsible. But I caused the fiasco at Friar Manor. I knew better than to betray him. I don't want to blame the drugs and alcohol on my behavior with you, but I couldn't stop myself. You told me then that I loved you and how I hadn't realized that myself. Why? Because you'd said, Kaine could be convincing."

And what she didn't say that she never loved Luka as he'd assumed. True her attraction to him grew to be supernatural, but she'd fallen in love with Kaine.

"Will he be able to convince you a second time?"

"I honestly can't say what is possible. Kaine's better, healthy, and he's made it clear to me he wants to rebuild our relationship. He's coming for me Luka, he's coming for … me."

Her words trailed to desperation because he'd already convinced her with his messages tucked in the guitar cases — she would leave with him.

She leaned in on Luka's chest, ashamed of her confession knowing it wounded him. She succumbed to Luka's strong embrace no longer able to hold back the tears any longer as she continued.

"Luka, I'm close to you. But I can't explain the feelings going on inside me. It scares me as much if not more than it does you." And she cautiously looked up to see what waited for her in his eyes.

No, no, she said in her mind.

Luka's eyes became a pinkish hue. She'd scared him more than she thought possible.

"Holly, I've planned to start a new life with you after Ian's wedding. I've told Tessa to expect divorce papers the first working day of the New Year. Holly, I want you for my wife if I haven't already lost you."

Well, he hadn't confessed he loved her, and for once, she was glad. But there were the words she'd feared.

Marry Luka, be his wife.

She no longer had an answer for him. She held on to Luka, knowing she was already gone, clinging, and crying out all her pain and confusion.

"Luka, I'm sorry. This wasn't the way ..." But she never finished her sentence.

Luka didn't want to listen to her betraying declaration, anyway. His mouth came quickly to hers and swallowed the final words. And when his anxiety lessened, he implored her.

"Let me take you and make you forget. Show you how I care. Holly, give me something to hold onto in my moments of doubt."

Luka picked her up and held her tightly. Her forehead lay cradled in the crook of his neck and carried her into their bedroom. He left the lights off, and the moonlight trickled in onto the dark, raspberry colored, chenille bedspread where Luka laid her down softly, gently as if he held a precious dissolving snowflake.

They helped each other off with their clothes while continuing to kiss.

She prepared to let go of Luka. He loved her with his body, his intent, and focused desire — to bring her back to him. She didn't believe he would succeed to pull her from the edge of the *Hurrikaine*. Luka loved her like a man who wouldn't lose this time. When her time arrived, she whispered, "Luka."

He didn't ask her to say it louder.

Tomorrow —Kaine

Holly awoke rested. Luka's tender lovemaking put her in a peaceful, gentle mood. There was never a doubt he loved her as she lay quietly in his arms.

A sharp pain seized her lower abdomen.

Chapter Twenty-Six

MEDICINE MAN

H olly held her breath. The pain stopped. Maybe it wasn't a cramp, and she'd overreacted. Relieved, but wary, she automatically cuddled into Luka's arms, while soft and melodic sounds of Indian flute music floated down the corridor. The beautiful song cast her thoughts adrift and then grew easy and then meditative. To add to her serene mood, the pungent scent of sage and lavender seeped into their room making the trancelike state even more surreal.

Luka quietly entered her and moved easily. She looked forward to it being the last time.

Later Trina met them at the breakfast table. After a lot of small talk over the preparation of oatmeal and sliced fruit, they drank the last of the freshly brewed pot of tea. Later Trina drove them an hour's distance to the Indian hot spring. The unspoiled landscape was equally breathtaking, pristine white and barren. And not one thought of her impending dilemma with Kaine entered her thoughts all morning.

Trina guided them along a wooded trail piled high with snow, passed trees whose limbs carried the pregnant burden of mounds of pure white snow. The vista before them spread out grandly bringing a mood of spiritually soothing and soulfully cleansing. They followed the banks of a frozen brook until they arrived at a clearing. There in the center, a sacred water pool bubbled with billowy white puffs of steam rising, inviting them to join the spirits of the past, present and future.

They followed Trina's lead after she stripped in the snow and laid her clothes on a rock under a plastic tarp. How mystical she looked when she walked closer to them, the mist circling her body, her hand stretched out to invite them. And without blinking her eyes, she boldly stood naked, saying a prayer to the four directions and to something, Holly couldn't see, and then stepped into the steamy waters up to her shoulders.

Holly glanced over to Luka. He shrugged his shoulders, and she saw his eyes sparkle ready for the adventure. Moments later, her body chilled, she stepped into the hundred-degree water and marveled at the contrast between sitting in the heated springs and the cold, icy temperature assaulting her face. Exactly like her predicament, being pulled in two extreme directions at once. Then she barred her thoughts on Kaine's imminent arrival.

Holly moved in the water nearer to Luka. His long angel hair dipped into the hot spring water and with three days growth of beard, caused him to look like a dreamy outlaw with his sky-blue eyes to-die-for. They were temporarily happy, thoughts of Kaine banished. They kissed freely in front of Trina until she complained about their honeymoon demeanor.

Trina laughed and threw a snowball at them, and a

rousing snowball fight broke out. And they laughed carefreely, deep soulful laughter, enjoying being together. Luka's eyes danced and sparkled every time he looked at her. She sat back absorbing the beauty of the fallen, crisp snow, lying like bolts of lace draped over the tree limbs while she took long deep breaths of the cold, heavy, pine-scented air. Moved by the hypnotic environment, she admitted to Trina.

"I can sense the sacredness of this place. I can see why the indigenous people keep this area a secret gathering spot."

"Yes," she heartily agreed. "If you're up for sacred rituals, I'll share one with you that may speak to your hearts when we return to my cabin."

The intrigue lured Holly and Luka.

"Yes, Trina." Luka volunteered.

"Tell us?"

Keeping the twinkle in her eye, Trina suggested.

"I'll show you when we get back, and we should be going soon. I don't want to get caught in a storm up here."

"You think a storm is blowing in today." Luka wondered aloud because the sky looked amazingly clear with giant billowing white clouds, a perfect day.

"Something big is brewing. An extremely powerful and destructive storm is coming. One we'll never forget." Trina predicted.

Exactly like a writer to drum up the drama with foreshadowing. But Holly sensed she was spot on because the storm the size of a *Hurrikaine* was coming and it headed toward her. She shook her head, dismissed the evil premonition, and fought Kaine back into the shadows of her mind. This day of relaxation with Luka needed to happen, and she would be damned if anything would spoil their final moments.

Trina made the drive back exciting filling it with more Indian legends and lore. Holly soon forgot about the storm a coming.

Another hour passed and settled in front of the fireplace, the three of them sat with their legs crossed in a circle, knees touching. Trina called it an Indian Pipe Ceremony and lit candles and placed sacred rocks and crystals all around them. She put on a CD of Native flute music to play softly in the background. And then she started to speak.

"What I have here is Sweet Grass, Cedar and Copal resin." She burned them on a circular brick of charcoal and smudged the black residue on each of their foreheads.

"We each take a turn pinching tobacco to offer up to Great Spirit. Then place it in the pipe and say a prayer. When we have all the tobacco in the pipe, we will each take a puff, holding the smoke in our mouths. Then we will release the smoke into the air. The smoke spreads, purifying our aura and clears out any negative vibes, carrying our supplications to the Great Spirit. This is a sacred and powerful ceremony. Please treat it with your utmost respect."

Holly and Luka agreed to the conditions. Trina started by requesting peace on Earth. Luka went next asking for protection for the planet. Holly followed with requesting good health to everyone.

When Luka took his turn, he sweetly whispered, "I request that first thing in the New Year that Holly becomes my wife."

Holly sat stunned by Luka's boldness. And again, Trina smiled a loving smile at Luka's ardent confession of love for Holly.

Luka passed the pipe to Holly.

How to respond?

Holly sat in a meditative state for a long while and then looked up into his waiting eyes. She placed the pinch of tobacco in the pipe and supplicated.

"I request the wisdom to know what is right."

The pipe passed to Trina then to Luka. "I'm respectfully asking that Holly will find it in her heart to forgive me and love me."

Without looking at her lobbied, "And stays with me."

He passed the pipe.

Luka's confidence grew bolder with each round, and his confessions agitated her.

Lost to confusing thoughts, time ceased to exist, but her next question rang clear and strong in her heart as she finally offered.

"I request a safe and long life for my future husband." She hesitantly looked at Luka's hopeful eyes and then she added, "... and for my child," as she placed her hand on the sacred life growing inside her. She turned her thoughts inward.

Please don't let Luka harm Kaine because of me. Please keep them both safe.

As a quick afterthought, added, *please let love, win.*

Holly released the dark, curling puffs of smoke encircle the room intertwining with Luka's smoke rings. It seemed unfair. He'd waded through months of hell with her. She'd spent less than a week with Kaine, but what a time. And at the end, Kaine loved her and was coming for her. She carried his child, and it was damn difficult.

And he was coming.

Kaine — coming for her — tomorrow.

olly sat exploring Luka's sad, blue eyes. Fear punctuated his usual sparkle. Trina's eyebrows lifted, the pregnancy obviously a piece of news to her. She nodded her head to acknowledge the forthcoming birth but being a wise woman, she kept a thousand questions to herself. She took custody of the pipe.

"I'm sorry, in light of the news of your child, I respectfully request that we end the ceremony. I don't want to the smoke to irritate you," Trina cautioned, then closed in prayer.

Holly watched Trina's swirls of jewel tones painted on her caftan disappear down the hallway leaving them alone. Luka turned to her, his crossed legs rubbing next to hers. She barely found the courage to look into his eyes. Eyes that loved her too.

He pulled her to him.

He spoke in a factual tone to comfort her.

"You're mine Holly Hill. I mean it, and as soon as the divorce goes through we'll be married." Luka pulled her into his arms hugging her.

She knew he would decide her silence meant she'd agreed.

But she didn't.

He added, "Don't worry about Kaine. I'll take care of him."

That's precisely what she feared, the possibility he'd meant more than looking out for him. She recalled the conversation in the canyon when Luka threatened.

I'll do something worse than put him in rehab.

Holly broke his embrace asking, "How much time do we have until it's time to catch our plane?"

"We need to pack. I'll get started." He kissed her on her cheek, then added. "Remember you're not alone."

Yes, Luka was worried. She observed how it whittling away at the seams of his confident smile. She wished she could split herself into and give herself to both of them.

She exhaled as she gazed out the window. The black thunderhead clouds looked heavy, bearing down unrelentingly, bending the giant boughs of the majestic trees. They bowed in respect to the power of the torrent wind meant to crush anything in its path.

She manically thought … Kaine … tomorrow.

Holly walked into the kitchen with a cold freeze in her bones. She paused, Trina stood quietly, stirring pancake batter, looking like she planned to say something.

"You know much about Luka?" Trina asked.

"Sometimes I do, then he does something out of left field, and I realize not at all."

"I understand that. Would it surprise you to learn Luka gave me, as a gift, the seed money to buy this house to devote myself exclusively to writing my screenplay? That he'd asked for little in return except that I do my best work. To have someone believe in me and give me exactly what I needed, was an amazing gift of trust, love, and support.

"Don't go getting any ideas. Luka's a brother to me. No funny business between us at any time during the past. I have a man I'm happy with creating a great life together. He's away, taking food and supplies to friends on the outer reservation due to the snowstorm. But I'm grateful to have this time with you, to share that Luka is a Superman. And yes, he has been known to jump tall buildings in a single bound."

They both joyously laughed at the mental picture.

"I've tried to pay Luka back the money he gave me to set up here, but he kept saying the smile on my face when I accepted the Oscar for the best original screenplay was payment enough. He's an unusual and special man Holly. Please know that."

The man Trina spoke of wasn't the Luka she'd been with for months. Skeptical, she cautiously asked. "Did Luka have anything to do with your film?"

"All he asked for was a credit as executive producer. At that point, he looked ahead to Hollywood, looking at his options and thought a credit might open a few doors. I was happy to reciprocate."

She'd bet he looked at options. And to end up with an Oscar for producing a screenplay would open more than a few doors in Hollywood. Everyone from the Hurrikaine camp told her that Luka always stockpiled a secret on them and to date, Trina's luck held, and he hadn't called in the favor … yet! What would it cost her when he did? Luka always thought of the future, and he did that with her future.

Trina turned away. It appeared as if she'd finished sharing her version of admiration and love for Luka. Then she confirmed.

"It looks like we're going to beat the storm to Albuquerque. But I'm not positive you're going to be able to catch your plane for L.A. They may be grounded."

And the spell of Luka broke.

She heard the calling. It became imperative she be on that plane.

Kaine was coming.

"That would be awful if we can't make our plane. We're expected in L.A., tomorrow."

"Luka told me. We can hope you're not slowed down by the storm at the airport." Trina paused. "Would it be terrible if you didn't catch that plane? What if you caught another plane and flew far away from Kaine?"

"You know?"

"Yes, Luka gave me a brief backstory yesterday at the hotel."

This was news enough, but there something else weighed on Trina's mind.

"I will guess he hasn't told you why we are close?"

Holly shook her head to say she didn't.

"I worked with *Hurrikaine* on their nineteen eighty-three, eighty-four world tour as Luka's executive assistant. Let me tell you, Luka attracted the girls like bees to golden honey. If you'll excuse the crassness of the phrase, he was fucked and sucked across the globe. But he never entertained any steadies."

Holly leaned over-the-counter cleaning up the trail of pancake batter and generally assisted getting the skillet ready trying to keep her hands busy. She needed Trina's story, another person speaking up for Luka like Catherine, Michael, and Jaden to balance the attacks from the Hurrikaine camp.

Holly glanced to Trina, shooting a look that said she waited for Trina's timely revelation.

"And?" Holly finally asked.

"Well, what I'm getting at is, Luka is crazy in love with you. And it's none of my business, but look how Kaine was tormenting the two of you. But, like I said, Luka's gone through women and never looked back. You're the first one he's ever introduced to me that claimed a last name."

Holly nodded, she'd been told that a few times.

"It's been a bizarre set of circumstances that brought Luka and me together."

"There's nothing bizarre about his being in love with you." Trina pointed out.

She poured the batter onto the hot grease. Soon small dots of dough quickly puffed up and popped. She flipped the cake and prepared another.

"In fact, I'm happy he's found, someone. He's been alone and lonely for a long time though I'm not positive he would admit it."

This story started to have a familiar ring to it. Who would believe these two beautiful and successful men, alone and lonely? How had it all happened?

"Luka's clever, intelligent and too handsome for his own good. Blend them with his charming English veneer, and as his friend, Holly, I'd hate to see Luka get fucked up, especially since he's finally put Carrin out of his heart and mind and trusts you.

"He's even willing to take on Kaine. Nobody needs Kaine. He's nothing but trouble. I've never seen him own a single solitary genuine feeling, and he's a master of manipulation. It's not easy being Kaine, but does he always have to act like an asshole?"

These past few months were different surrounded by people that either loved or admired Luka. Not like the *Hurrikaine* camp that constantly tore him to shreds with mistrust and malicious accusations. But she'd seen for herself that the thin veneer Trina spoke about threatening to crack. She stacked the pancakes as Trina cooked them onto their separate plates.

"Luka tells me Kaine has fallen in love with you too. That Kaine has changed."

Holly's stomach knotted, *not again*, she thought, *not again*. What's fucking special about her? That these two usually non-committal, hell-raising men should be unable to live without her? Holly's greatest fear surfaced once again. This is a contest, and she the prize.

"Trina, this may sound paranoid, but sometimes I wonder if there's a chance that I'm a pawn in a diabolical game fought in their subconscious. It's like neither realizes how much they once loved each other to be and be filled to the brim with anger at each other."

"That is a bit paranoid. However, there's a bit of truth. Once they were closer than most brothers were. Each like a beautiful wild stallion kicking the fence down needing more freedom. Together they fought all the challenges the world threw at them. And together they beat the odds.

"They are a brilliant, unbeatable team when they operate together. Full of spirit and fire, and that's to be admired.

"You see how Luka thinks, always another deal around the corner. Well, Kaine to his credit is an equal match. He kept the products flowing for Luka to distribute. They became the perfect business team. And as skilled a musician, as Luka is, he accepted Kaine as the star and stepped back. Kaine possessed the power and charisma for Luka to sell, at any cost. And it came to be.

"But Luka's business savvy proved to have no limits. Kaine agreed, and they kicked down the fence railings, setting them free from the stagnant music industry until the old standards resembled a pile of sawdust, or, maybe a pile of toothpicks.

"Luka called me on Thanksgiving to wish me a happy holiday and excited about closing the deal of the century. And as a close trusted friend, he wanted me to stand by in case he needed me. I'd do anything for Luka, and he knows that."

Holly admired Trina's unwavering loyalty. Luka moved amongst his people freely and always wore his power lightly. And knowing his intention to become the most powerful man in the music industry impressed her. She remembered long ago at her introduction to him, and Howard said all she ever needed to know, *Oh no My Lady, he IS CMT*. Luka, the man in the trenches inspiring loyalty, made many rich and others a household name.

The lightning struck, and she realized what Luka meant. *Worse than rehab.*

Luka might stop the *Hurrikaine* phenomena on CMT. CMT owned the cable rights to the whole tour. He'd ended the career of many once powerful stars. Hadn't it happened when CMT stopped playing the heavy metal music in favor of alternative music? Where were the stars of the eighties?

Yes, Luka could stop Kaine, and it would be worse than rehab. Could this be the final piece of business with Kaine, for Luka to take it all back? All of what Luka originally owned — the music, the money, now the girl, and lastly Kaine's life. *I'll own him*, he'd once said.

Trina pulled out a jar of apricot preserves and dabbed a spoonful on top of each stack of cakes.

"What do you think goes on every day you're with Luka? Haven't you read the tabloids? The press mills have been horrible to Kaine in Europe. The tabloids supplied the world, documented, blow-by-blow details, of his losing you to Luka.

"And not to defend him, because he is a prick, they went after Kaine's blood. They watched him fall apart after the nude photos of you and Luka surfaced on the cover of all the rags in Europe. Your every move with Luka is noted and photographed in every tabloid on the planet. What will it do to Luka to lose you to Kaine, again, in front of the whole world? Haven't enough people been damaged?"

"Why me?" Holly muttered under her breath, not wanting to be held responsible for anyone being unhappy. Nothing was simple anymore.

"I can say," Trina consoled. "You have what they both never found and are fighting each other, for you ... your love."

How true Trina's words, Holly thought.

And the dim scene replayed quietly in the back of her mind. Luka and Kaine fought on the way to the airport, the morning they all left London. That forced Luka's hand, and he quit the tour and brought Holly home.

Trina's knife hit the cutting board harshly as she sliced an orange in halves for the juicer.

Trina continued, "For the first time Luka would have it all. He left *Hurrikaine* to work for CMT, and that move made Kaine go mad and broke up the partnership. But Luka told me he'd finished with touring, but he wanted to stay in the music industry and was looking for a deal.

"He wanted to get in on something big, but out and away from *Hurrikaine*. Then, as I said, at Thanksgiving he called to say he'd found the deal he'd been looking for to make a killing."

Holly took the plates of pancakes to set on the dining table as Trina ran the juicer.

Luka walked in at that moment. His sunny smile slightly marred with curiosity.

"What have the pair of you been chin wagging about so early?"

"You, of course," Trina affirmed with a teasing tone.

"I hope you haven't had a go at me and set Holly against me with tales of my torrid youth?"

Trina laughed. "It certainly was a torrid youth."

Holly smiled.

"She's been telling me what a wonderful friend you've been to her." Holly walked over and placed her arms around his shoulders and hugged him dearly.

"I don't think your reputation could take finding out how nice you are, Poppa Bear."

He smiled, squeezed her quickly reflecting her endearment, and dropped a kiss on her lips.

"No, you don't Luka Hunter," Trina protested. "You

leave her alone, sit, and have a good lunch!" Trina wore the look of, 'don't start that lovebird stuff again', but seemed secretly pleased to see Luka happy.

Later that afternoon, Trina drove with great caution down the snowy mountainside. Their conversations filled with comments wondering if the plane would take off on time. But their luck didn't hold.

And Trina's words haunted Holly.

Would it be terrible if you didn't catch that plane and went the other direction, away from Kaine?

Why did planes forever defining her world?

The snowstorm hit remorseless and demanding forcing planes to remain grounded, and the hotels filled quickly. The three shared a large suite and spent an unforgivably uncomfortable night in an airport hotel next to the Albuquerque International Airport waiting out the blizzard. She'd been resting in the hotel bedroom when a persistent cramp seized her abdomen.

She sat up instantly alarmed.

She could not lose this child!

And then it happened again.

The moment she recognized it wasn't a cramp but the kick of life from her child. Kaine's child. She turned to Luka, moments from initiating his nightly routine with her. But she couldn't. Not now! Not ever again! Luka could never touch her again. Not after having life move inside her. It was one thing to think cognitively that she was pregnant, but quite another to feel the first pangs of her child alive, moving, she and Kaine's child!

That ended Luka.

Come what may, she would never share her body with him — ever again.

She turned to Luka.

He saw it in her eyes, "No? Then let me hold you."

He understood — he'd lost her.

Holly fell asleep in Luka's arms wandering around in torturous dreams of Luka and Kaine constantly smashing each other's faces.

Kaine — Today

Holly affectionately bid goodbye to Trina, promising to remember everything she told her and to call if she needed moral support. She was a true friend to Luka. Trina turned and headed back to her mountain nest, confident Holly would love Luka as he deserved.

Holly and Luka spent the morning entertaining themselves by picking out names for the baby. She hadn't the heart to tell him their father already named them. Storm for his son and Savanna for his daughter.

Luka insisted that as soon as the authorities served his divorce papers he would announce their engagement.

His efforts were useless — she would leave with Kaine.

The sun hung straight up in the gray sky as Holly sat strapped into the plane that carried her closer to the eye of the *Hurrikaine*. Her worried facial expression must have said it all.

Chapter Twenty-Eight

OUR LOVES IN JEOPARDY

December 30, 1989

B y mid-afternoon, Holly staggered down the brick steps to her house and of course, standing at attention against her front door, three guitar cases awaiting her inspection. She scooped them up and walked to her place where the musty scent of dried roses mixed with the Christmas pine created a divinely fragrant potpourri perfuming the air.

With no time to check the notes from Kaine, she quickly sat the latest testaments of Kaine's eternal love inside her closet. Then walked over to the large, expensive gift from Kaine delivered Christmas Eve.

Luka bounded in, drenched from the sheet of rain, her luggage in his hands. She shook the rain from them and set them next to the exit. With minutes to repack, they headed for Pasadena, where the pre-wedding rituals were already in full swing.

The unrelenting weather waited patiently for her arrival in California, by taming itself to thunder and lightning storm, the likes she'd never experienced. Her lack of restful sleep and the outstanding fact that Kaine, expected in mere hours — her nerves were shattered.

When a crackling flash of lightning tore the pregnant sky in half, it startled her, sending her running frightened into Luka's soothing arms. Holly stood nestled in Luka's embrace, his hand stroking her hair, calming her. But he was anything but calm. His heart pounded fast, and not due to arousal, he wasn't even half-aroused.

Holly started to pull away.

Luka pleaded, "No, don't. Please. Let me hold you. This is the last time I can hold you without...." He paused and looked down into her eyes.

She drifted in his soft, warm, familiar blue eyes that stayed with her through Hell, and his reflected an equally exhausted and on edge man. She took a deep breath and spoke the name they both dreaded.

"Without Kaine."

She took her hands and slipped them inside his warm wool lined Levi jacket and squeezed his trim waist tight as he lovingly hugged her in return.

She looked up again.

"I may have lost you, but you will never leave me," he said firmly. His lips came close to hers bringing the scent of peppermint to caress her senses.

Holly hadn't decided if her lips would kiss his. He'd calmly threatened her again.

You will never leave me.

The steadfast words ricocheted about in her mind as she

awaited his tongue. She closed her eyes, took a deep breath, then relaxed, relieved for the final goodbye. She drew him into her mouth positive she'd never love him again.

As she continued to kiss Luka, thoughts of Kaine's imminent arrival started to torment her.

Then the kick of life happened again.

She'd taken enough, stopped kissing him, and stepped away.

Kaine — it was a matter of time.

Chapter Twenty-Nine

I REMEMBER YOU

Holly stepped away — due to Luka's diabolical confessions. Too many filled with deceit and hatred. He was a dangerous man. She needed to hold on a few more hours to avoid his wrath because then he would hate her too like he did Kaine. She decided not to imagine what his revenge on her would be.

Her resentment erupted again due to his latest threat. She pulled Luka closer to protect her change of heart and not alert him. She took her hands from behind his back, ran them up to his neck, into his long soft, rain-damp hair, and confidently stated. "Luka, don't worry my angel-eyed man about Kaine. I can take care of him."

Luka studied her eyes, the doubt spreading quickly.

"If you don't, I will," he promised with a deliberate tone.

Holly squashed her anxieties, she'd been right on the money to pretend that his admission hadn't unsettled her.

Luka walked her backward until the back of her legs brushed against her bed.

He stopped. "Babe, you're my dream come true. And

I'm going to show you how much I do care about you and our future, to ensure you'll never forget!"

She nodded....

Luka turned away from her, leaving her sitting on the edge of the bed. His eyes said he'd understood the doubt even though clear about Kaine. And that as a pragmatic man, there could be a possibility this might be their last moments together. He put on *The Healers* CD and pushed repeat. When he turned around, he'd lost his sparkle. He wasn't aroused.

They both knew everything headed toward the finale. And the moment became punctuated by the lightning cutting deep and invincible, while the thunder followed, roaring, persuading all below to run for cover, announcing the storms arrived.

Luka moved quickly, sat beside her, took her into his arms, and leaned her back on the bed, but he was not aroused. He wrapped his body around hers and promised.

"After the wedding tomorrow, everything will be wonderful. You and I can be married, and we can live in L.A., or anywhere you want to raise the baby. Or if you wish live in Santa Barbara, you would be close to your parents."

Holly rested in his arms, the safe refuge she'd known for oh, so long. She lovingly placed her hand on his warm cheek, her heart sad for him. He'd been a man looking for a second chance to redeem himself, grow into a man he wanted to be proud of and bury his past with its ugly secrets and demons.

But she wasn't the woman to walk that path with him. She held back the tears of sorrow making sure not to confuse him, by allowing him to believe she cried happy tears at his vision of their future together.

Luka's familiar hands caressed her body with a thirst and tenderness of a longtime lover. Soon he would want her naked.

Holly moved slowly, concerned that he would sense her withdrawal from him. She'd never make love with him the same day she would see Kaine.

She moved... struggling against his resistance to letting her go.

"Luka, I'm sorry. I have a splitting headache."

"Then have a bit of a lie down here. Rest till half past, it's going to be a long night."

Luka held her, occasionally kissing her with kisses she didn't want or his sweet passion and dedicated affection. But he didn't press, his hands lightly caressed her lovingly, softly and gentle yet attentive to every detail.

As a sign of the end, the storm exploded overhead and fell in blankets of rain drenching everything around her home. The lightning crashed, and the thunder rolled up and over her cottage.

Between breaths, he pledged.

"You're mine, Babe ... till death do us part..."

TO BE CONTINUED...

Dear Reader,

Please take a moment and leave a few comments about your favorite scenes wherever you purchased *LIAISON*. It is crucial to the series to have immediate feedback while the pleasure from the story is fresh in your mind. Thank you for your valuable support. YOU ROCK!

The Shattering Truth...

A black storm is following Holly Hill. Landfall promises to bring destruction and no one is safe. She is anxious and filled with intrepidation as she anticipates the arrival of dark haired poet, Kaine Walker, rock star. Will Holly be able to free herself from the powerful hold that Luka Hunter has on her and follow her heart?

The Evil Lies...

Luka Hunter's plan is working flawlessly. He is confident and waiting for the perfect moment to spring a big surprise on Holly. Will it bring joy, heartbreak, or vengeance?

To Be Revealed...

Kaine Walker is expected and everyone is on edge predicting the outcome of his inevitable confrontation with Luka Hunter. Will his presence bring love or death? No matter, which, he will cause devastation like no one has ever seen.

Time is running out...
Who can she trust?

http://www.kewtownsend.com/

KEW TOWNSEND

Affairs of the Heart ~ London Series

HEART (Part 1), **TEMPTATION** (Part 2)
PROMISES (Part 3), **DEVOTED** (Part 4), **BETRAYAL** (Part 5)

Affairs of the Heart ~ Hollywood Series

BLOOD (Part 1), **SURRENDER** (Part 2),
DECEPTION (Part 4)

Ms. Townsend is a widow with a wonderful daughter, educator of school-age students, travel and movie buff, and writes romantic music fiction set in the 1960s-1980s rock scene in the *Affairs of the Heart Series*. She lives in sunny Southern California and loves to read under a palm tree with wave's crashing along the shoreline.

KEW's love of rock music started at a young age when she returned glass Coke bottles for change to buy 45 rpm records. Her interest moved from the music to the musicians, and living in Hollywood, interviewed the Beatles when they landed at Los Angeles International Airport. Acquiring a taste for the funny Englishmen, she started dating one of the Rolling Stones that exposed her to sex, drugs, and rock and roll. Later her memories surfaced in the *Affairs of the Heart Series* where she weaves her behind the scenes anecdotes with her long love of castles, mysteries, lightning, and thunder into a romantic suspense story. Her master's degree in Cultural Anthropology and Archaeology adds to her world travels, and flavor to her novels.

CONTACT KEW
kewtownsend.com

Leave a message, a review, and sign up for NEWSLETTER. Be first to hear about new releases, preorders, sales, prizes, giveaways, and fun events.

www.ingramcontent.com/pod-product-compliance
Lightning Source LLC
Chambersburg PA
CBHW050026180626
46810CB00002B/594